**'This isn't fai...
come waltzi...
disrupt things...'**

Maybe her words were harsh, but she could hear the pleading in her voice. 'There's never been anything more than a casual fling between us, and I can't do that here.'

'Why not?' he asked, as he bent his head to kiss her again.

Lauren put up a hand to stop him. 'In a country town no one's business is private. This is my home town, my life. Where on earth could anything between us go?'

'Why do we have to have it all worked out right now?'

She looked away, but he put two fingers beneath her chin and tilted her head up gently, forcing her to meet his gaze. 'You don't really think it's over between us. The way you kissed me just now proves that...'

Emily Forbes is actually two sisters who share a passion for reading and a love of writing. Currently living three minutes apart in South Australia, with their husbands and young families, they saw writing for Medical Romance™ as the ideal opportunity to switch careers. They come from a medical family, and between them have degrees in physiotherapy, psychology, law and business. With this background they were drawn to the Medical Romance series, first as readers and now also as writers. Their shared interests include travel, cooking, photography and languages.

Recent titles by the same author:

THE CONSULTANT'S TEMPTATION

CITY DOCTOR, OUTBACK NURSE

BY
EMILY FORBES

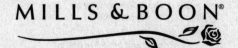

MILLS & BOON®

To our husbands, with love—
thank you for your support and encouragement

All the characters in this book have no existence outside the imagination of the author, and have no relation whatsoever to anyone bearing the same name or names. They are not even distantly inspired by any individual known or unknown to the author, and all the incidents are pure invention.

First published in Great Britain 2004
Harlequin Mills & Boon Limited,
Eton House, 18-24 Paradise Road, Richmond, Surrey TW9 1SR

© Emily Forbes 2004

ISBN 0 263 83929 X

Set in Times Roman 10½ on 12 pt.
03-1004-49729

Printed and bound in Spain
by Litografia Rosés, S.A., Barcelona

CHAPTER ONE

'HOLY Moly.' Lauren raised her hand against the midday sun and squinted at the figure striding across the tarmac from the Air Ambulance Service headquarters towards them. 'Of all the airports, in all the countries—'

'I don't think you've got that quote quite right,' interrupted Ryan as he turned and looked back down the steps of the plane. 'Who's that?'

'Someone I never expected to see out here.' She was sure it was him. Jack Montgomery, A and E specialist. But he was supposed to be in Canada, and Canada was about as far from outback Australia as you could get. Maybe she was mistaken.

No. She'd recognise that loping stride anywhere, the confident air and the tilt of his handsome head. Her heart was hammering in her chest, her mouth was dry and her palms were damp. No one else had ever affected her in this way.

Lauren rubbed her hands on her trousers as Jack reached the plane. She was still standing on the bottom step and their eyes were level, bright blue meeting dark chocolate brown in an unblinking gaze.

'Hello, Lauren.' He looked her dead in the eye, a smile on his lips, and if he was surprised to see her, she certainly couldn't see the signs.

She stepped down onto the tarmac. She had to do *something* to break eye contact, break the spell.

'Jack. This is a surprise. What brings you out here?' Her voice sounded cool to her own ears, which made no sense because there was no reason to be unhappy with him. Not really.

'I'm your medical officer. Sheila in your office said to come straight out and hitch a ride. Might as well get straight into it.'

Lauren felt her jaw drop. 'You can't be our new doctor.'

Ryan was more welcoming, extending a hand in greeting. 'So you're Jack Montgomery. Welcome to the team. I'm Ryan Fitzpatrick, one of the pilots.'

'You *knew* he was coming? Why didn't you tell me?'

'The other doctor pulled out at the last minute and Jack stepped in. I just assumed you knew that.' He looked from Lauren to Jack, then back again, but if he'd been going to ask any questions he obviously decided against it. 'You guys can sort it out on the flight. We've got to get going.'

Ryan motioned for Jack to board first. He held Lauren back for a moment. 'You can tell me how you know him tonight.'

He winked at her, and Lauren was relieved that he could make a joke of the situation. Ryan didn't have a claim on her, not really, not now, but that wouldn't have stopped other men from being jealous in this same situation.

On board, she took longer than she needed with her seat belt. It was easier than confronting the fact that her past had just walked into her present. And future, too, if Jack was here to work. With one smile and a few words, suddenly her stomach was full of butterflies and she was having trouble remembering what she was doing.

'You need some help with that?'

Lauren looked up at Jack and saw the sparkle in his dark eyes. She laughed and some of the tension dispelled.

'No, I'm about right. I'd better filll you in on what we're heading for.' She hesitated. 'And maybe when we're back at the base, you can fill me in on what you're doing here.'

Jack nodded. 'Sure.' He leant back in his seat as the eight-person plane started to taxi down the runway.

Lauren waited until they were in the air before speaking. They were seated side by side with the aisle between them, but even with that barrier of space Lauren felt the familiar kick in her stomach when she turned in her seat and saw his strong profile, dark against the sunlight streaming through the small window. It was still there, that almost tangible pull between them, and she'd better learn to ignore it. Fast. She'd had the best weeks of her life with that man but that was all in the past now. She wasn't putting herself through the heartache of the aftermath again. Keeping her mind on work was imperative. 'How much do you know about procedure and the sort of things we do at the Air Ambulance Service?'

'Enough to go on with. What have we got now?'

Typical Jack, sure of himself and straight to the point. Both were valuable qualities in the outback service the AAS provided. Operating under conditions of isolation, the nurses and doctors had to be able to make quick, appropriate decisions in difficult conditions. He'd probably be a help rather than a hindrance, in the job at least. Her personal life might be another matter entirely.

'Fourteen-year-old male with facial injuries. He came off his motorbike on his parents' property and tangled with a barbed-wire fence. I'm not sure of the extent of his injuries, but according to his dad there's a lot of blood and a deep wound near the left eye. The call came through a few minutes before you arrived.'

He nodded, a little frown creasing his brow as he took

in her explanation and her matter-of-fact tone. 'I realise you wouldn't normally need a doctor for a case like this, so call it orientation for me if it makes you feel better. Like I said, Sheila said to come straight out and it seemed like a good way to get my finger on the pulse.' He smiled again and the butterflies in her stomach started fluttering anew. 'Where are we headed?'

'A sheep station about a twenty-minute flight north-west from here.' Lauren paused and squinted across at Jack. 'How long is your contract?'

'How do you know I'm on contract?' Jack's lean face was serious.

'City boys like you don't take up permanent posts in the country. The guy you're taking over from was only here for eighteen months and my bet is you're here for a lot less than that.'

'Is that a problem?'

She shrugged. 'It affects the level of care we provide when our medicos don't stay for long. They just get the hang of it, then they're off. It's a common problem out here.'

'Then I'll have to make myself useful from day one and earn my keep.'

'You do that, Jack Montgomery, and we might even have something nice to say about you when you're gone.' It was a pity he was so likable and straightforward. No doubt people really would be singing his praises long after he left, and she'd just have to grin and bear it.

Lauren grabbed a medical kit and was off the plane as soon as Ryan lowered the steps, motioning with a hand over her head for Jack to follow her to a ute that was waiting on the edge of the airstrip.

The driver leant over to release the doorhandle. 'Hop

in.' They crammed into the front seat to drive to the homestead, a small collection of buildings on a dusty flat a few hundred metres away. 'Thanks for getting here so quickly. I'm Pete, Brad's dad.' He accelerated away as he spoke, and in a matter of seconds they were at the house. 'Brad's in here with his mum, Peg.'

As they entered the house, cool air washed over them and Lauren squinted into the room, dark after the glare outside. They greeted Peg and then Jack stood back as Lauren went to Brad, lying on the couch.

'Hi, Brad, my name is Lauren. I'm a flight nurse.' She appreciated that Jack hadn't tried to take over. They were in her territory now and he seemed to respect that. She turned and waved a hand in his direction. 'That's Dr Montgomery, our newest flying doctor. What have you been doing to yourself today?' Lauren sounded both efficient and calming despite feeling anything but. She could feel Jack's eyes on her and it was throwing her into a spin. What was he thinking, coming here? She forced herself to concentrate as she realised Pete was speaking to her.

'We were rounding up sheep when one decided to go its own way—you know how stupid sheep can be.' She murmured in agreement. Her parents ran a sheep station and she knew from first-hand experience how dumb sheep were. 'Brad changed direction to avoid colliding with the sheep but there was a fence right next to him. He couldn't stop in time and ran straight into the wire.'

Peg interrupted. 'Normally we wouldn't have bothered to call you but it's such a nasty wound that I didn't think we should make a five-hour round trip to town.'

Lauren squatted down next to the patient and gently removed the blood-soaked towel he was holding to his cheek. 'You did the right thing, Peg,' she said. 'This is going to take some fancy sewing. Jack, will you take a look, please?' She also knew which one of them was best for the job.

She turned around as she spoke and her pulse quickened as she looked up at Jack, leaning against the wall. He walked across to her and her eyes took in his long lean legs, encased in sand-coloured chinos, and slim hips. She knew that under his white shirt his abdominal muscles ran in taut creases across his body and she remembered, as if it were yesterday, how the golden brown skin became paler a few centimetres below his waist. She blew out a slow breath and tried not to jump as he squatted beside her, his thigh touching hers.

She watched as he made a quick but thorough assessment of Brad's injury. He was confident, but then this was hardly a challenge to an experienced A and E specialist.

'You've done a good job on yourself,' Jack said. The barbed wire had sliced into Brad's skin, making a jagged incision from above his left eyelid across to his ear. 'The worst thing about barbed wire is that it doesn't give a nice neat cut. The edges are quite rough and it makes stitching the wound together more difficult. I'm no plastic surgeon but I'm pretty sure I can put you back together.'

Brad lay on the couch, eyes closed, face pale.

Lauren could see the wire had cut quite deeply into the muscle surrounding the eye and that Jack was checking for nerve damage.

'Can you squeeze your eyes tightly closed for me, just for a second?'

Brad did as asked but his expression showed how painful it was.

'Well done.' He turned to her. 'The nerve's intact. Would you draw up some local anaesthetic, please?'

His voice was professional, impersonal even, but the deep tones still sent a thrill through her.

'It doesn't appear that the nerve has been damaged so I can stitch you up now,' Jack explained to Brad. 'I'm going to give you a couple of injections. Both are anaesthetics, just to make sure that I numb all the area.'

Lauren bent over the medical kit, starting to gather the items he'd need, glad to have something to do. Something other than watch Jack be great at his work and gorgeous to look at.

'I want the finest gauge needle that we have for suturing.'

That voice! She'd never have believed she could go weak at the knees just because a man had requested a needle for suturing. 'Do you want…' She stopped to clear her throat, her voice seemed to be as affected as her knees. 'Dissolving or regular?'

'Dissolving is fine for the muscle but regular will leave less of a scar for the external sutures so give me both.'

She'd never seen Jack treating patients before. He was impressive in the way he gave explanations for his decisions. So far, so good. Medically speaking. But she'd been right to be worried about the impact he'd have on her.

She passed him the first needle and stepped aside to give him maximum light, watching as he checked the area was numb, then went to work with total concentration and a steady hand. He made small stitches and she doubted Brad would have much scarring. Each time Jack finished a section of stitches he nodded to Lauren, who snipped the end of the thread. They worked in complete silence for thirty minutes. Lauren kept her focus on the job before them but she was still aware of Jack beside her.

The final stitch in place, Jack turned to her with a wink and a smile that made her catch her breath. The corners of his eyes crinkled and she well remembered that grin. Full of cheek and an unassuming confidence in himself, she'd had no defences against it all those months ago. He'd been here for less than three hours and already it was clear that the time apart hadn't strengthened her immunity to his charms.

He removed his gloves. 'Good work. Can you fashion up a waterproof dressing for this young man?'

'Of course.' Her reply was brief. She was still recovering from that smile. Her reaction just didn't make sense. He was completely wrong for her. Their lives were as opposite as could be and she'd left all memories of him behind in Adelaide.

'He'll need a tetanus shot and some antibiotics as well. He's not allergic to anything, is he?' Jack checked with Peg.

'Only tidying up his room,' she joked.

'I think he can be excused from that chore for a while now.' Jack laughed and Brad's parents joined in, relieved to share a joke now that the drama was over.

Lauren thought, not for the first time, how amazing it was that people out here bounced back so quickly from shock.

Jack was busy issuing further instructions. 'He'll need to come to town in a week for the stitches to be removed. Keep it dry until then and make sure he finishes the course of antibiotics. I don't want any infection. Any concerns, make sure you ring us, OK?'

Ten minutes later they were back on the plane, taxiing down the runway.

'Thanks for trusting me with that big important role

back there.' He was smiling and her knees turned to jelly again. 'Do you throw all your new doctors in the deep end like that?'

'Too much for you, big shot?' She looked out her window, watching as the arid land fell away from them, not prepared to look at him for too long in case he smiled at her again. She saw movement on the sands below. 'Look, emus. Out your window. We're flying right over them.'

They watched in silence until they'd left behind the sight of the big birds tearing across the desert. He'd hit her for a six when he'd appeared out of the blue, but she would handle this. She'd be nice, be natural, keep hold of her feelings.

Ryan's voice came through the intercom. 'Sheila's on the radio for you, Lauren.'

She hopped out of her seat and walked the few paces to the cockpit, calling back to Jack, 'Bye-bye, cup of coffee.' She slid into the seat next to Ryan in the tiny cockpit and placed the headphones over her ears.

'Hi, Sheila, what have you got for us?'

'An MVA, single car. Sounds like it hit some loose stones and lost control. We'll need both you and Jack so you'll fly straight there if Jack's happy. It'll be an orientation day to remember but we'll save time if you don't have to head back here to pick up Matt.'

'That'll be fine.' Lauren called Jack up to the cockpit and handed him a set of headphones, filling him in on the call-out as Ryan got more details.

'We're not far away now. What's been organised for landing?'

'There were two people in the car following behind. One's at the accident site to hold back any traffic and the driver has gone one and a half kilometres north to stop traffic approaching. That gives you a clear run for landing. The road's wide enough and it's bitumen.'

'No problem.'

'Jack's with me now—what can we expect?'

Sheila filled them in and Lauren thought it only fair to add a warning to Jack before he returned to his seat. 'Make sure your seat belt's fastened.'

Jack raised an eyebrow at her in silent query.

'We're in for an interesting landing. Try and enjoy it, it'll be something to e-mail your friends about.' She laughed as his narrowed gaze and the set of his mouth showed he wasn't quite certain what to make of her comment. 'I'll stay up here in case Ryan needs an extra pair of eyes.' She grinned at him. 'And you can relax and enjoy the ride.'

Within minutes, Ryan was bringing the plane around, checking the scene below before approaching for landing. Jack could see glimpses of the rolled vehicle and the tyre marks showing how the driver had overcorrected after running onto the verge, swinging back across the road and rolling off the other side. He knew it could be messy but his thoughts were interrupted by the bump of the plane landing on the road, tyres screeching on the bitumen. He shook his head. Would this strange new world he'd walked into seem normal in a week or two?

Ryan taxied towards the accident site, covering the few hundred metres slowly. Once stopped, he wasted no time before getting the plane's steps in place.

'Take one of these.'

Jack took the medical kit Lauren was holding out to him and she led the way down the steps, moving towards the car. The heat was burning up from the ground as much as from the sun above them.

They stopped next to the dark green sedan, its crumpled roof testament to it having done a full roll before landing on its wheels again. Jack and Lauren peered through the smashed windows. The female driver was covered in fine white powder, the residue from the activated airbag sticking to the blood on her face and arms. Her head was resting back on the seat and she was holding the right side of her chest. Her eyes were closed but she was talking faintly to two children in the back seat. The children, a baby and a toddler, were still restrained in their special seats, crying heartily.

Jack forced open the badly dented door. 'I'm Jack, the flying doctor. Can you hear me?' The woman nodded. 'Everything's going to be OK. Can you tell me your name?'

'Loretta.' Her answer was a whisper.

'Good. Are those your children in the back?'

Another nod. 'Toby and Julia.'

Jack turned to Lauren as he pulled on a pair of gloves. 'Can you get the children out while I check Loretta?'

Lauren prised open the rear door opposite the toddler, whose crying had lessened with their arrival but wasn't about to stop completely. The baby was also still crying but Lauren spied a dummy pinned to her top. Slipping this into her mouth quieted her immediately and gave them some respite from the noise. The baby was in a capsule so Lauren removed the carry basket from the car, passing it out to Ryan. She was halfway round to the other side of the car when Jack's voice stopped her in her tracks.

'I need help here. Now.' Jack had a stethoscope pressed against Loretta's chest. 'Probable tension pneumothorax. We need to do a chest decompression. Pass me a scalpel.' Lauren delved into the medical kit and withdrew the instrument and an alcoholic swab.

She watched as he felt below Loretta's right clavicle, palpating expertly for the intercostal space between the second and third ribs. 'Needle, 12-gauge.' She'd anticipated this request and had it ready. Locating the intercostal space, Jack swabbed the area then pierced the skin and muscle into the pleural cavity around the collapsed lung, deftly inserting the needle as Lauren exchanged it for the scalpel. The air hissed as it escaped from the chest cavity and out through the large-bore needle.

Without waiting to be asked, Lauren strapped an oxygen mask over Loretta's nose and mouth and hung the oxygen cylinder over the door. Jack nodded his thanks but kept talking to his patient.

'OK, Loretta, you've fractured some ribs and that's done some damage. You had air in your chest, which was stopping your lungs from inflating, that's why you had trouble breathing. You'll be OK now but I need to leave this needle in your side as a temporary measure.'

'My kids?'

Jack looked to Lauren for confirmation and when she nodded, he replied, 'They're fine. I need to finish checking you over.'

'Toby?' Lauren mouthed the question to Jack who nodded. Lauren flew around to the toddler's seat to check him and get him out of the car before Jack needed her assistance again.

Toby's cries had subsided to loud sobs. Lauren's assessment was as thorough as she could manage on a squirming, crying toddler. Apart from a large contusion on the left side of his head, possibly from hitting his head against the window, he appeared uninjured.

'Let's get you out of the car.' Lauren undid his harness, careful not to let go of him in case he tried to clamber between the front seats to his mother. Holding him around his waist, she lifted him out of his seat and passed him to Ryan. Strictly speaking, helping with the medical care wasn't in the pilot's job description but out here they often needed an extra pair of capable hands. A drink bottle lay on the floor of the car and Lauren reached for it, thinking that it might help to calm Toby.

'Dammit,' she swore as her shoulder hit the doorframe when she twisted around to climb out of the car.

'You OK?' Ryan flicked a glance at her.

'Yes.' She could hardly say otherwise in the scheme of things. Jack didn't take his attention off his patient and Lauren felt a frisson of annoyance that she couldn't quite explain. It was totally ridiculous to suggest that she wanted Jack's sympathy, particularly when he was busy with a patient.

'Ready when you are, Lauren,' Jack called.

She passed Toby's drink to Ryan. 'Here's his bottle. Looks like it's juice or cordial so it'll be good for shock.'

Jack started talking as soon as Lauren arrived at his side. 'No other major injuries that I can find but we'll use the spinal board to transfer Loretta to the stretcher.'

Together they slid Loretta out of the car and onto the stretcher, hooking the oxygen to the side.

Ryan carried Toby over, the little boy sucking his drink as he clung to Ryan's side like a monkey. 'There's your mum. She's just having a rest.'

Ryan's voice carried back to them as he carried Toby away. 'How would you like to fly in that shiny plane over there?'

Jack was ready to transfer Loretta. He looked up to find Lauren. She was smiling with pure delight, her face radiant. Jack thought she'd never looked more beautiful but his heart plummeted when he saw she was smiling at Ryan. 'Lauren.' Good, at least he had her attention now. 'We need to get Loretta into the plane.'

A tiny frown crossed her face but it disappeared just as quickly, and Jack guessed she'd attributed his impatience purely to concern for Loretta. Together they picked up the stretcher and Lauren showed him how to operate the automatic winch to lift it into the plane. Once the stretcher was secured, running down one side of the aisle in place of three rows of single seats, Ryan handed Toby to Jack so he could get ready for take-off.

The moment Toby was handed over, he began to howl in protest. Jack successfully distracted him, making little duck sounds that had Toby looking all around for the source of the noise.

'Do you do horses?'

He turned to the seat behind him where Lauren was busy with the baby. 'I do a great horse. But I only do requests on special occasions.'

She clipped the seat belt back around the capsule and moved to crouch in the aisle by Jack. 'You've never landed on a road before, so that's quite an occasion.'

He laughed softly, and their eyes met. 'Yes, it is.'

Lauren's smile grew as Toby started tugging on Jack's collar. 'Horsie, horsie!'

'Looks like Toby got lucky today,' she said, as Jack did as requested. 'You and Ryan both have a knack with children.' She stood up as Ryan announced over the intercom that they were ready for take-off and rumpled the top of Toby's blond head before walking back down the aisle to her seat.

Jack's hopes that they'd covered some ground, made some progress towards getting back what they'd had in Adelaide, took a nosedive as he replayed her comments on his touch with children. Comparing him and Ryan like that was hardly a compliment. Not that he had anything against Ryan—he seemed like a great guy—but Ryan was her *friend*, no one special. Or was he something more?

He'd come here to see if he and Lauren could continue what they'd started all those months ago. It hadn't occurred to him she might not be available, that her life might have moved on. Maybe that had been arrogant. Maybe it had been wishful thinking. What *was* the story with her and Ryan? Had she compared them because she saw them both in the same light? Colleagues? Friends?

They were in the air now and the noise from the engine, far from upsetting Toby, had him nodding off on Jack's lap. Jack breathed a sigh of relief. The thought of a distraught toddler screaming on his lap had crossed his mind as a possibility. Baby Julia was another matter. She'd woken up and was crying softly. Lauren moved up to her and took her out of the capsule, soothing her with gentle shushing noises until she was quiet. He heard Lauren fasten Julia back into the capsule and cross over to take Loretta's obs again. Once she finished, she filled in her notes, then turned to him, and somehow he wasn't embarrassed to have been caught out watching her. Neither of them looked away.

And he knew. Whatever had been between them was there still. He held her gaze, a thousand words spoken with no sound, a single look taking them both back in time, and for an instant the months that had gone by vanished as if they'd never happened. They were back six months ago when the world, for a few short weeks, had ceased to exist, and it had just been the two of them. The memories of those days and nights came flooding back, transporting them to what they'd thought only a brief episode, a snapshot of two people crossing paths for a moment in time. So fleeting, so wonderful, they'd both thrown caution to the winds and seized the moment. Jack reached out to her, couldn't take his eyes off her as she moved towards him slowly, and his every nerve ending screamed with memory.

Then Ryan coughed.

Jack saw how Lauren's gaze flew straight to the cockpit and how she froze like a rabbit caught in the glare of headlights. A flush of colour, possibly guilt, swept over her face. He knew now that he still affected her as much as she affected him. But there were complications he hadn't been counting on. And it looked as though the biggest complication might be the man flying their plane.

CHAPTER TWO

'How was that landing?' Lauren asked Jack as their plane taxied towards the AAS headquarters.

They were the first words either of them had spoken since Ryan had coughed and Lauren had returned to her seat, meeting Jack's eyes only for an instant.

'Better,' he replied, undoing his seat belt as the plane came to a halt.

The door opened, bright sunlight spilling into the plane's interior. Matt, the on-call medical officer who Jack had met earlier, appeared, motioning to him. 'Give me a hand to take the stretcher out.' Together they unloaded the stretcher into the waiting ambulance.

'What's the procedure now?'

'Any patients we retrieve and admit into the hospital are kept under our care. We have visiting rights there. We need to check if yours have been granted, otherwise they'll go on my list.' Returning to the plane, Matt saw Toby standing in the doorway. 'OK, little fellow, let's get you inside.' He grasped him under the arms, swinging him down. Kerry, the hospital's social worker, was waiting and took Toby's hand. Lauren emerged next, cradling baby Julia.

'I'll take the children to the hospital and admit them for observation. I'll look after them there until their dad arrives,' Kerry said.

As Lauren went to hand the baby over, Julia scrunched up her little face and started to squirm and cry. At the noise, her big brother's bottom lip began to tremble and a single tear slid down his face.

Lauren took one look at them both, pulled the baby back against her chest and said to Kerry, 'I'm coming with you. At least until you get them settled.'

Ryan put his hand on her shoulder. 'I'll pick you up from the hospital and drop you home. Just give me a call when you're about done.'

'Thanks, but I'll still need to come back to the base to file my report.'

'No problem.'

Jack caught the end of the conversation as he returned from the office.

'Whose patient is she going to be?' Matt asked him.

With his thoughts still on Lauren it took Jack a moment to realise that Matt was talking about the injured mum. 'Mine,' he replied. 'Sheila just needed my signature on the paperwork and now I'm all set. I'll ride in the ambulance.'

Lauren sat on one of the wooden benches that flanked the main entrance to the Port Cadney District Hospital. The late afternoon sunshine was still hot and she turned her face away from it, eyes closed as she waited for Ryan. How would he react when he found out just how well she and Jack knew each other?

She'd never said anything to him about her time in Adelaide, telling herself when she'd come home it was all in the past. Which, of course, it was. Jack's arrival in Port Cadney didn't mean anything. It was just a coincidence that he was here. They had agreed on the terms of the affair and rekindling old passions was not on the agenda.

'Still here?'

Lauren jumped as she heard Jack's voice. Her eyes flew open and landed on him immediately. Her heart somersaulted as he smiled at her. Even when he was serious he was devastatingly handsome, but she doubted there was a woman alive who wouldn't be blindsided when he smiled. 'I'm waiting for Ryan. Where are you heading?'

'I was hoping to find a taxi. My bags are still out at the airport.'

'Sit down and wait with me.' She waved a hand at the seat. 'We'll give you a lift. I have to go back to the base, too, and write my report.' Lauren attempted a smile but it felt less than natural.

'Sure it's no trouble?'

'What? Having you sit next to me or giving you a lift?' At least if she established a pattern of joking with him, that would keep other thoughts at bay. It was how she and her colleagues generally interacted so treating him the same seemed the best plan of action. And, right now, it was her only one.

'You tell me.'

'I think I can be trusted not to rip your clothes off in broad daylight,' she teased.

Jack laughed. 'Damn. I was hoping you'd still find me irresistible.' He had a mischievous twinkle in his eye, one of the things that Lauren had found hard to resist.

'What do you mean—still?'

'Lauren…' Jack's words were drowned out by a loud toot. Ryan had pulled into the car park at the end of the path and was yelling out of his window.

'Ready to go?'

'Jack needs a lift back to the base.'

'Hop in. Are you all right to get back to town later?'

Jack nodded. 'Apparently there's a car waiting for me at the airport.'

Lauren offered Jack the front seat and was content to sit in the back, listening as Ryan pointed out some landmarks around the town. Sitting out of sight, she could study Jack. His short, dark hair was flecked with silver, more so than she remembered, but it suited him. As he turned his head now and again to look out of the window, she could see his face. A perfectly proportioned profile with a straight nose. Smoothly shaven, no stubble to obscure the strong lines of his jaw or the dimple in his right cheek that came and went as he spoke.

What was it about him that got her so excited? Her heart never leapt when she saw Ryan but then, she'd known Ryan her whole life. Was that the difference? Maybe it was the twinkle in Jack's eye, hinting at hidden mischief. Or was it the challenge he presented? He was, after all, from a different world to hers and she knew those two worlds could never mesh.

'Do you want to meet us for beer and pizza at about nine-thirty?' Ryan was asking Jack as she tuned into their conversation. 'We've got tennis tonight and we all grab dinner afterwards.'

'I don't think—'

'I'm sure Jack will be too tired,' Lauren interrupted. Country hospitality was one thing, but to have her ex-boyfriend become mates with an ex-lover was just too weird. Especially when she didn't even know why Jack was here. Her world had been rocked by his appearance today and she needed some time to process this development.

'On second thoughts, I think I will. I'm not at all tired. Thanks.'

Lauren glared at the back of his head until he turned

to look at her. He'd been about to decline when she'd cut him off too quickly, throwing him a challenge. She'd have to remember that and practise lying low. He smiled triumphantly and she struggled to continue scowling.

Jack had no trouble finding the local pizzeria. Red and white check cloths on the tables and the Chianti bottles in the window were almost universal indicators. His empty stomach growled in anticipation as he walked through the door. There was a pleasant garlicky smell in the air and he hoped the food lived up to the promise. Searching the crowded room, looking for a familiar face, he saw Lauren walking across the room.

Her dark hair was pulled into a ponytail and her cheeks were flushed with warmth. She was wearing a fleecy jacket but her legs were bare. Jack could just make out the hem of her tennis skirt but that hardly registered. All he could do was stare at her amazing legs, long and brown, slender and toned. She stopped at a table and her sudden halt brought Jack's eyes up again. He dragged his attention away as Ryan spotted him and waved an arm over his head, yelling, 'Oi! Over here.' All heads at the table turned in his direction for a second before conversation resumed, leaving him to make his way through the tight-packed tables.

He dodged chairs and legs, people and tables, with each step conscious that he was walking into Lauren's world and that the people he was about to meet were her friends. What they thought of him mattered. At least, it would do once word got out that he wanted Lauren.

It felt strange, caring what others would think of him. It was a long time since it had occurred to him to think about how anyone else saw him. He was Jack Montgomery, A and E specialist, dedicated to his work and undeniably good at it. He was respected by his peers and emulated by his juniors, all of whom he kept at a safe distance, personally speaking. He took all this for granted, and so it was doubly strange now to find himself on trial in a way.

Lauren's friends didn't yet know anything about him, but this first meeting would set the scene for their later opinions. And opinions there would be. He might be a city boy, but even in the city friends could be vicious in their defence of one another when it came to a potential suitor. And what was the stereotype in the country? 'We look after our own.' Where had he heard that? He couldn't remember, but it was like a warning call to be on his best behaviour and make a good impression. Wouldn't his colleagues chuckle now if they could see him feeling as self-conscious as a kid on a first date?

He concentrated on keeping his eyes off Lauren. It was Ryan who'd invited him and Lauren's reaction in the car had shown she didn't second the invitation.

Ryan stood to shake his hand and make the introductions, but before he started, Lauren, still standing at the foot of the table, said, 'I'm just going to get the first round. I'll get you something to drink if you like.'

Chilly. The others at the table didn't seem to twig that the temperature had just dropped a few degrees. Other, perhaps, than Ryan? Jack saw him look closely at Lauren just for a second, as if that was all he needed to check out what was up with her. Or it might just have been his imagination working overtime.

'A light beer, thanks. Whatever's on tap is fine.'

Lauren gave a curt nod and raised her voice, asking, 'Any last orders?' before walking off with long strides to the bar as Ryan started on the introductions.

'Jack, meet Chloe, Lauren's flatmate and an AAS

nurse, and Connor, my brother and a local paramedic. This is Jack Montgomery, our newest doctor.'

'Welcome.'

'Nice to meet you.'

Connor and Chloe spoke in unison as Connor reached over to shake his hand.

Jack forced himself to focus, to file away names with matching faces, to try to work out who was with whom, if anyone was paired up at all, and generally make himself agreeable. Which shouldn't have been that hard. He was Mr Agreeable himself when he didn't really care what impression he made. But that's when it came naturally. Now, when it counted, he felt the pressure.

Besides, his mind was already in two other places. Lauren. And the possibility of something going on between Lauren and Ryan. He still didn't know the lie of the land as far as they went, and the last thing he wanted was to step on any toes, declare an interest in someone who was already taken. But he hated to think that he might be out of the running for Lauren's affections on day one, before he'd even got out of the blocks. He hadn't come here to lose. In fact, it hadn't occurred to him that losing was even an option. Years in A and E didn't leave much room for self-doubt. Maybe his confidence had seeped over into his personal life, but at least he knew what he wanted.

'Do you play tennis, Jack?'

Petite, blonde. That was…Clarissa? No, Chloe. Jeez, he was more out of sorts than he'd thought. She patted the empty seat next to her and he sat down, aware she was looking at him with more interest than just that of a friendly face welcoming a newcomer to town.

'Now and again. I'm not sure I'm in form at the moment.'

Chloe pouted. She did it prettily, as though if he could only snap his fingers and have his tennis up to scratch, it would make her day. But it was the opposite of what Lauren would do and it left him unmoved. Where *was* Lauren?

Chloe wasn't finished yet. 'Have you come from Adelaide, Jack?'

He dragged his attention back to her. 'Originally, but I've just got home from Canada.'

'I bet that was fabulous. Did you go skiing?'

'I didn't have time. I was working.'

If Chloe thought Jack's reply was rather brief she showed no sign of it. 'On what?'

'Disaster evacuation procedures. I'm in A and E.'

'So what brings you here?'

Lauren.

But he wasn't giving his agenda away just yet. 'I want to learn the ropes with the AAS. There's nothing else like this in the world.' Then, before Chloe had a chance to ask any more questions, he changed the topic back to something safer, focused on her. 'How did your tennis go tonight?'

Ryan seemed to take this as a cue to join their conversation, which was fine by Jack.

'Our team won convincingly. Lauren won both her sets as usual, and we won as well,' he said, indicating that he was talking about Chloe.

'Is it mixed doubles?'

Chloe answered. 'Four of us to a team. We each play two sets of mixed doubles, swapping partners for the second set. Connor and I let the side down tonight.'

'It's only a bit of fun,' Ryan added. 'We're not playing for sheep stations.'

'Only a bit of fun!' She was back. 'Ryan Fitzpatrick,

I can't believe you said that. What's the point in playing if you're not trying to win?' There were two vacant chairs at the table and she slid into the one furthest from Jack.

Ryan rolled his eyes in mock exasperation. 'Not everyone has the same killer instinct as you.'

'I bet you don't complain when we win the tournament on Saturday.'

'All I know is that I'm thankful to be playing on the same side of the net as you and not having to return your shots.'

Lauren poked her tongue out at Ryan as the others laughed.

'What tournament is this?' Jack wanted to know.

'Just an AAS fundraiser,' Ryan said. 'Lauren makes it sound like the Australian Open.'

'It's a great day,' Chloe said. 'Tennis matches in the afternoon followed by a dinner dance at the country club. You should come.'

'I rather think I'd have to, seeing I'm now an AAS employee,' Jack replied.

The pizzas were placed in the centre of the table, cutting short Jack's reply, and Connor waved a hand at the spread. 'Help yourself, Jack. Don't be shy or you'll miss out.'

'Smells terrific,' said Jack. 'The kitchen facilities in the hospital accommodation aren't too flash. I thought I might be in danger of starving.'

'The accommodation is convenient but that's about all you can say,' Chloe said. 'I couldn't wait to get out of there.'

'You've stayed there?' Jack asked, taking a slice of pizza from the tray Ryan was holding and placing a slice on Chloe's plate when she nodded. He was distracted for a moment when he sensed a tidal wave of cool vibes from Lauren's side of the table, but he resisted the urge to look at her.

'I moved here from country New South Wales about six months ago and bunked down at the hospital. Luckily Lauren needed a flatmate soon after so now I share with her.'

As the pizza was devoured and more drinks ordered, Lauren tried not to listen as Jack and Chloe started chatting about how Chloe had settled in. It was doing her no good at all. In fact, she could feel herself turning green with envy. Although Chloe was usually as ready for fun as Lauren, she was also a lot of things Lauren wasn't. Tiny and blonde. Chloe laughed daintily and never drank beer. None of that had ever bothered her before but right now Lauren was fighting off a number of uncharitable thoughts towards her friend. She chomped into a piece of pizza and tried to tune them out, but her eyes kept returning to Jack. All the other men in the room paled in comparison. No one seemed as tall, as fit or as good-looking. Jack had a presence, an unassuming confidence. Combined with his physical attractiveness, he set a high standard.

'Lauren, isn't there a vacant unit in our complex? I'm sure the owners would give Jack a short-term lease.' Chloe's question interrupted her daydreaming and she almost choked on an anchovy.

Jack Montgomery living next door! No way. She aimed for nonchalance. 'I don't think so, I haven't seen anyone move out.'

'I'm positive number three is empty. I'll check it out if you like.' Chloe had already turned away from Lauren and was giving Jack her full attention again.

'You're unusually quiet.'

Lauren quickly shuttered her thoughts when Ryan spoke. Having virtually grown up together he could read her too easily and she didn't want anyone getting inside her head until she'd figured things out for herself. 'Just tired. Busy day.'

'More drinks, anyone?' Chloe interrupted.

'One more, thanks,' said Ryan. 'I'm rostered off for the next few days.'

'Me, too,' Chloe said. 'Lauren?'

'No, I'm working tomorrow. I really should be going.'

'In that case...' Ryan said, as he pushed his chair away from the table.

'It's OK, you stay. I can walk home.' Lauren pre-empted Ryan's offer to accompany her. She wanted to be alone.

'I can give you a lift. I'm about to head off.' Jack was already standing, shrugging on his jacket.

'My unit is literally around the corner, Jack. I'll see you guys later.' She bolted for the door, leaving Jack to say his goodbyes, but she could still hear Chloe promising to call him about the unit in their block.

Lying in her bed an hour later, Lauren imagined having Jack living next door. She'd spent six months trying to get him out of her system. She thought she'd managed quite well until the exact minute she'd seen him again in the flesh. All the memories had come flooding back. The way his eyes creased when he broke into his devilish grin, the way he'd always held doors open for her and seated her first at a table. The way his hands had warmed her skin and how soft his lips were. His taste and smell, his warm scent which would envelop her when they woke in each other's arms. She couldn't bear the pain of sep-aration all over again and he was a city boy just as surely as she was a country girl. He would leave, she didn't doubt that for a minute.

Maybe his arrival here was pure coincidence. Maybe he wasn't interested in rekindling their affair. But what if he was?

Could she trust herself not to run to him if he called? She certainly hadn't put up much resistance the first time. But back then her motto had been 'Life is short' and she'd always seized any opportunity with both hands. But that had been then.

And now? Now she knew better. She'd experienced the emptiness that had swamped her when she and Jack had parted, and she'd learnt from that. Now she was no longer sure that diving in without sparing a thought for the consequences was always the wisest decision. At least, not where Jack was concerned.

Lauren still wasn't ready to face the world the next morning. What she really wanted to do was drive out to her parents' farm for some solitude. Take her horse for a ride and work out how she was going to deal with Jack working in Port Cadney. She should be able to manage. They had made a mutual decision, an adult decision regarding their affair, and now she needed to behave in an adult manner.

But she'd also answered her question from last night, the question that had been buzzing around in her head when she'd fallen asleep. She couldn't trust herself where Jack was concerned. She'd been fooling herself, thinking he was out of her system. It was going to be hard to keep her reaction to him under wraps.

Forty minutes later she was towel-drying her hair when her mobile phone rang. She cursed under her breath as she picked it up, not at all prepared to go out on a flight.

'Good morning, Lauren.'

'Jack.' Just hearing his voice was enough to start her heart racing and leave her feeling slightly breathless. *I am not going to let him affect me like this, I am not, I am not.* But as hard as she tried to conjure up distracting images, all she could see were Jack's dark eyes with the mischievous twinkle, his broad shoulders and his smile. Especially his smile. And that dimple. Not to mention his skilful hands and his well-muscled biceps. The list was indecently long. Did she really stand a snowflake's chance in hell of resisting him?

'What are you doing?' he asked.

Lauren looked down at her naked body, phone in one hand, towel in the other, and blurted out the truth before her brain kicked into gear.

'You got me out of the shower.'

'Are you alone?'

Lauren paused before answering but no answer seemed right. 'Perhaps.'

She heard Jack's sharp intake of breath. 'Hell, Lauren.'

So she *did* still affect him, too. 'Did you want something?'

'You're the on-call nurse today, aren't you, not the clinic nurse?'

'I hope so, otherwise I've missed the plane.'

'I was just wondering what you do here when you're on call.'

She didn't believe him for a minute but at least work was a safe topic so she seized it. 'Bored already? I imagine we do the same things you did in the city. Catch up with friends, housework, check in at the hospital.'

'What do you have planned for today?'

Lauren tucked the phone against her shoulder while she wrapped the towel around her, a smile on her lips.

'I'm sorting out my sock drawer. Would you like to help?'

'I'd better not. People might get the wrong idea.'

'I was joking.' He'd thrown her. Annoying. She'd been off balance since his arrival and it didn't look as if things were going improve in a hurry.

'I know.' He laughed, a rich, deep sound that washed over her. 'I'm at the hospital. I thought if you were coming here we could catch up for a coffee.'

So that was the real reason for his call. Maybe his arrival in town wasn't so innocent.

Or maybe he was simply asking her for coffee. 'You're at the hospital already?'

'I called in to see Loretta.'

'How's she doing?'

'Pretty well. Waiting for her lung to re-expand fully so she's still got the drain *in situ*. It will be a while before she goes home to her two small children but she's in good spirits. She's lucky we got to her as fast as we did.'

Lauren could hear the note of pride in Jack's voice and it pleased her—on a professional level, of course. She felt the same way when a job had been completed successfully. Their work was an invaluable part of the outback community and Lauren was proud to be part of the team. A team that had no equivalent in the city.

It was only showing Jack some country hospitality, and she'd do the same for any newcomer, so she agreed. 'I'll see you in twenty.'

Half an hour later Lauren was questioning the wisdom of voluntarily spending time with Jack. As they walked beside each other down the passageways, skirting barouches, basins and visitors, their arms brushed against each other, sending shivers of excitement coursing through her. It was hardly the location for great passion-ate reactions so what would she feel like if they were somewhere more private?

They walked out into the sunshine and Lauren put some distance between them. Coming towards them along the path was a young girl, pushing a baby in a pram.

'Another one,' Jack said.

'Another what?'

'Teenage mother. She must be the fifth one I've seen this morning.'

'There's a newborn health clinic at the hospital today.'

'Specifically for babies of teenage mothers?'

'Not to my knowledge,' Lauren replied, 'but that's not a bad idea.' She had a soft spot for young mothers. 'One of her causes,' as her father said.

'There seem to be a lot of young mothers here.'

'It's the country.'

'What do you mean by that?'

'Things are different here. Once these kids finish their education, having children is often the next step in life.'

'What about their careers?'

'This is the *country*, Jack. There aren't a lot of big career options unless they're prepared to move away. Lots of them are happy just having a job. Working in a trade or on one of the farms or fishing boats is a good, honest way to earn a living.'

'So they finish school, get a job, get married and have babies. All done by the age of twenty-five?'

'It doesn't work out quite that well for all of them but for some that's the case. It's not necessarily a bad thing.' Jack was a city boy and had certainly never struggled to find employment so she didn't expect him to automatically understand. 'Haven't you ever done anything without planning it all first?' Lauren took his silence as confirmation of her suspicions. 'I didn't think so. It might be hard for you to comprehend, but sometimes things just happen.'

'You're not speaking from experience.' It was a comment, not a question.

'No. Teen pregnancy is just a hobby of mine.'

'Hobby?'

'I run a social group for teenage mothers.'

'In your spare time.'

'Mmm.' Not quite in her spare time but that was just semantics.

'Why the interest?'

'For some of these girls their pregnancy was unplanned and they've made a tough decision to keep their babies. They don't all have good support networks and those girls in particular need a community around them. Being a mother isn't easy and it can be doubly hard if you're young or single.'

'I agree it would be a tough decision but it's one they *have* made and should be able to support.'

Lauren swallowed her impatience. Just. 'Opportunities in the country are limited. These girls need our support to build their self-esteem.'

'That's not what—'

'It's something I'm passionate about.' Jack opened his mouth again but she wasn't giving him a chance to speak. 'And committed to.'

'But—'

'And it's not your place to comment on social issues in this town when you've only been here for five minutes.'

'Lauren—'

'I don't think I'll have that coffee after all. I'll see you at work.'

She turned on her heel and left without a backward glance, trying to shake the image of Jack's bewildered expression.

She strode through the streets, trying to calm down. Could she really have misjudged his character so badly? She had a tendency to think the best of people but Jack was a decent person. She hadn't been wrong about him, had she? He was a doctor after all. Surely he had to have some compassion.

She reached her destination and hammered on Ryan's door. He was barely awake but that didn't stop her bombarding him with the details of her latest drama.

Eventually she paused for breath and he took his chance. 'I don't know what history the two of you share but you'll have to find a way of working with him.' He paused but when she didn't volunteer any information, he continued. 'You know how important a harmonious work environment is within the AAS. It's high pressure enough without having the two of you at loggerheads.'

'Somebody needs to set him straight.'

Ryan raised his hands in front of him like a shield. 'Don't look at me! Just because his opinion differs from yours doesn't make him a bad person or necessarily wrong. Did he actually say that your groups are a bad idea or that the mums don't need our support?'

'No.'

'Are you sure you're not a bit peeved just because he dared to have an opinion of his own?' Lauren glared at him in reply. 'He seems like an intelligent bloke. If it means this much to you, you'll have to try and educate him.'

'What do you suggest I do?'

'Invite him to one of your clinics.'

'That might be a good idea,' she said as her mobile rang. 'I'll think about it.'

She answered the call.

'Lauren, it's Sheila. We've got a suspected ectopic pregnancy. It's Rachel Fraser, and I need you here for a retrieval.'

'On my way.'

Lauren walked out to the aircraft after a quick briefing from Sheila. Settling herself into the copilot's seat next to Steve, her face fell when she saw Jack climbing into a passenger seat behind her.

'What are you doing?'

'Coming along for the ride. I'm not needed at the base.'

You're not needed here either, she thought, but said nothing, reaching for the headset instead so she had an excuse not to talk to him. Even though she was furious with him, her heart didn't seem to remember and was somersaulting in her chest.

'Lauren, are you there?' Sheila's voice came through the headset.

'Yes.'

'Roger Fraser, Rachel's husband, is on the radio. Can you take over?'

'Sure. Patch him through.'

Lauren could feel Jack's eyes on her, even as she concentrated on the call. The small plane felt claustrophobic today, the tension thick in the air.

'Roger, it's Lauren. How's Rachel doing?'

'She said the pain's getting worse, she's not sure how much more she can stand. I feel so helpless. I've never seen her like this, not even when she went into labour with Bobby.'

'You can give Rachel some pethidine for the pain—you should have some ampoules in your medical box. Can you find one?'

Lauren could hear Roger rummaging in the box. Each outlying station had a well-equipped medical box, replenished by the AAS for emergency use.

'Got it.' She heard the relief in Roger's voice.

'Good. How much does Rachel weigh?' Lauren spoke loudly against the noise of the engine as Steve revved for take off.

'Sixty-four kilograms.' Rachel's voice came faintly through the phone.

'OK. Roger, find a new syringe and draw up 75 milligrams.' Lauren waited.

'There's nowhere to put the needle in.'

'You have to snap the vial open, twist the neck of the ampoule.'

'Oh, I see.'

'Do it carefully,' she instructed.

Lauren heard the snap and then Roger said, 'Seventy-five milligrams, OK?'

'Well done.' She made her voice rich with encouragement but she was tense. Talking someone through a medical procedure, even one as simple as this, always made her nervous. And Jack being here wasn't helping. 'Just inject it into Rachel's muscle, either the top of her leg or her bottom will do. She should feel better in a few minutes.'

'Thanks.'

'No problem. We're on our way now. Can you get Rachel out to the airstrip once the pain relief kicks in? It'll speed things up.'

'No worries.'

'Great, we'll see you in about forty minutes but we'll be in radio contact if you need us.' Lauren hoped they would make it before Rachel's Fallopian tube ruptured, which was the risk if the diagnosis was correct.

On arrival, Lauren concentrated on Rachel, aware of Jack's constant presence as she assessed her patient, kneeling next to her on the back seat of the car. At least he had the good sense to remain quiet while he observed everything, including her. She purposefully ignored him but it took a lot of effort. Reaching into the medical kit, her hand brushed against his leg. Through the thin cotton of his pants she could feel the muscle of his thigh and a shiver of excitement passed through her. She could hear him breathing from where he stood behind her and she could imagine his warm breath on her neck. The slightest contact, the tiniest reminder, brought alive all the memories she'd fought so hard to bury. A touch, a sound, a scent—they all seemed to tap straight into her subconscious, a subconscious filled with recollections of Jack.

Lauren shook her head and continued to palpate Rachel's abdomen. By the time she'd completed her examination she'd decided it was safe to transfer Rachel. With Jack's help Rachel was settled onto the stretcher and lifted into the plane.

Lauren chose a seat next to Rachel, behind Jack. Jack's attitude was disappointing but this argument was a godsend. Staying angry with him would help her get through the next few months. She'd have to come to some sort of truce for the sake of their work, but if she could keep her distance, keep a lid on those memories, it'd go a long way to overriding her body's treacherous reactions to him.

Connor Fitzpatrick was waiting with the ambulance to transfer Rachel to the hospital. Once that had been done Lauren was grateful to have a few minutes to herself with the justification that she needed to tidy the plane. Pivoting in the doorway, she collided with Jack's broad chest. Automatically she put her hands up to protect herself but found her right hand directly over his heart, the strong beat pulsing under her fingers. She tried to push herself away but Jack held her hands firmly but gently against his chest.

'Lauren, I'm sorry if I upset you.' His voice was a caress. Sincere and caring. She felt like a heel, or a child, carrying on the dispute unnecessarily. But when he spoke to her like that she knew she was in danger of falling for him all over again.

'Are you?'

'I realise I'm new in town and there are probably things I don't understand, but I think you're assuming things about me. Putting words in my mouth.'

She wasn't ready to let him off the hook just yet. It'd be plain stupid to do that. 'Am I? It's a shame you won't be around long enough to prove yourself.' Lauren pulled her hand away and Jack let it go. She tried not to notice the emptiness she felt once contact was broken. 'If you'll excuse me, I need to straighten up in here.' Her tone didn't invite further conversation.

Jack left, walking across the tarmac without a backward glance. Lauren stood watching his easy, loping gait, the things she needed to do forgotten. This wasn't how it was meant to work. She never had the tables turned on her, she always won arguments. So why did she feel she was not only losing the fight, she was losing the whole battle? She held fast to the handle inside the door, restraining herself from running after him, the ache in her chest threatening to overwhelm her as she watched his retreating figure, shoulders set, his head high, his stride long and purposeful. He looked like a man with a mission, whereas she felt like she'd been dragged through a bush backwards and then flung in a heap.

CHAPTER THREE

THWACK. Lauren hit the ball with all her force and felt satisfaction flood through her, tinged with guilt when she saw Ryan duck to avoid being struck in the face by it.

'Steady on, Lauren, you're meant to be playing tennis, not collecting heads.'

Lauren laughed. 'I'm just getting started.' She pulled another ball from the pocket of her fitted orange shorts and threw it high just in front of her. Her serve was fast and accurate and she knew there was no chance of Ryan returning it.

'Yes!' Lauren punched the air seconds later as Ryan lunged after the ball, falling onto the court and missing the shot, making it her fifth ace in as many games. It was a few seconds before she realised Ryan was still lying on the court.

She ran and leapt the net, clearing it easily, and stopped by Ryan's side. 'Are you OK?'

'No, you wretch, I've twisted my ankle.'

'I'll help you up. You can hop over to the sideline and I'll grab an icepack from the club in a sec.' Seeing Jack walking towards them from the country club, she called out, 'We've got our first injury of the day.' He probably wanted to ignore her after her outburst yesterday but he wouldn't do that, with Ryan watching. He was too much of a gentleman. 'Could you bring me an icepack?'

Jack returned with the requested cold pack. 'You OK, Ryan? Need a hand?'

'I could have done with one when Lauren was busy

wiping me off the court, literally.' He winced as Lauren wrapped the frozen bag around his ankle, already slightly swollen.

'Seems you take your tennis pretty seriously.'

Lauren looked up as Jack spoke, but Ryan answered before she could figure out whether she'd just been criticised.

Ryan shook his head. 'The woman's crazy.'

Lauren grinned. 'Knowing me as you do, I'd say you were crazy to take me on.'

'I *wasn't* taking you on. We're down as partners in the tournament. This was just a warm-up, which is not, I repeat *not*, about killing people.'

'Are you any kinder on your real opponents?' She saw Jack smiling down at her, and Lauren wished she'd kept her focus on Ryan's rather hairy ankle instead, a passion-killer for sure. A warm tremor rushed through her body the moment she met Jack's eyes. He was standing next to her, Ryan on her other side. Jack was close enough to smell and she couldn't help herself. Before she knew it she'd breathed in deep and filled her head with the spicy male scent of him. It was like a drug and she let her eyes flutter closed as she drew in another long slow breath.

'Easy does it. You don't want to maim me and then cut off my circulation, too.'

'What?'

'My ankle, you're squeezing it so hard my foot'll drop off.'

'Don't be a baby,' Lauren said, but she released the pressure on Ryan's ankle and chided herself, That's why work and fantasy life don't mix.

'You treat your patients with the same brute force you use on the court, I see.' Jack had slipped his hands in his pockets, looking for all the world as if he was enjoying the show. Lauren ignored him.

'You playing? You're all dressed for it,' Ryan said.

If he'd picked up on the tension he was doing a good job of ignoring it.

'No, the teams were already signed up. I'm just here to watch and fill in if needed.'

'Looks like you're playing now. Lauren's short a partner.'

'Hold on there, don't go fixing me up with partners.'

Jack was looking hard at her, a frown etched deep into his forehead. Damn, but he was sexy when he did that. She was kneeling on the ground now, holding the ice firm over Ryan's ankle. Jack's groin was just inches above her head. He was in white tennis shorts that ended just high enough on his lean thighs to be teasing but just low enough to be decent. Manly. The fabric and cut were both classic, no slogans splashed across them. They'd make an odd pair on the court, her in her form-fitting clash of pink and orange, so why not? It didn't mean they had to be nice to each other.

'OK.' Lauren stood up to face Jack, and Ryan quickly grabbed the icepack to keep it on.

'Pardon?'

'You've got yourself a partner. Can you play?'

'Of course I can play!'

Lauren held her hands up in mock-protection. 'Just checking. Keep your pants on.' She grinned as an image filled her head. Then frowned as she remembered it was not good form to fantasise about a colleague's naked body. Particularly when Ryan, right next to her, knew her so well he could almost read her mind.

Lauren and Jack walked off the court and into the country club for a cold drink and a shower after winning the doubles final. Lauren's gait was light next to Jack's and he was very aware of how fresh she still seemed, as if three solid hours of tennis was all in a day's work for her. Then again, it might be. Maybe she and Ryan hung out here all the time. Maybe it was one of their favourite couple activities. He shook his head to get rid of the image. It wasn't a safe place to go.

Ryan greeted them. 'Glad to see I'm not the only one who can't keep up with the women around here.'

'It's vicious out there. Why didn't you warn me?' Jack had revived somewhat and although he knew he'd be stiff and sore tomorrow, his mind was now firmly on Ryan. He wasn't sure he had Ryan's relationship with Lauren worked out and he needed to know what he was up against.

'Thought you'd have figured it out by now. Country women take no prisoners. And she's a good few years younger than you, too. At least I have youth on my side.'

Jack laughed but then wondered whether there'd been a warning in Ryan's words. How much had Lauren told him about their time together in Adelaide? She was certainly unusually quiet—distracted? His attention was piqued as he saw Ryan tap her shoulder.

'I won't come on to dinner. I need to keep this ankle up if I'm going to be back at work in forty-eight hours.'

'OK. I'll walk you out.'

They all stood up at the same time and Ryan wrapped his arm around Lauren's shoulders, leaning on her as they walked slowly off to the exit. Jack breathed a sigh of relief. Now he'd have time with Lauren away from work and away from Ryan. Maybe the gods were looking out for him after all.

*   *   *

Lauren entered the dining room, having stopped to shower and change after seeing Ryan off. Her gaze landed on Jack the instant she walked in. His shoulders were broad and strong in his linen shirt and the nape of his neck, brown and solid, was just visible above his collar.

She didn't want him. Couldn't. Shouldn't.

OK, so she had to admit there was some meaningless attraction between them, but at the end of the day that didn't count for anything. He was all wrong for her. Hadn't he shown that when she'd known him before? They wanted different things out of life and he was a threat to her dreams, just like her father had been for her mother's. If she needed any more proof of that, hadn't he provided it tenfold with his attitude toward teenage mothers? She stifled the little voice in her head that argued she'd never actually let him explain his views.

'Be flippant and keep him distant. Don't let him under your skin,' she murmured to herself as she approached the table and slid into the chair reserved for her next to Jack.

Ryan's place had already been removed and all the seats were full. The noise was impressive and it would only get louder as the beer and wine flowed freely all night. She was in no danger of giving in to her attraction to him here at least. There was safety in numbers. They'd had fun on the court, she'd been so focused on the game that she'd let other issues rest, but she had every intention of resurrecting her earlier stance. There was safety in that, too.

Jack seemed to have other ideas about what would be safe. The moment she sat down, he turned towards her. 'I guess we'll have to be pleasant to one another now we're dinner partners.' He was smiling, hard to resist, but

Lauren decided not to let the argument between them disappear just like that. It was one of her safety mechanisms.

'We're work partners, too, but that didn't make you pleasant the other day.'

'I've already apologised for that. I had no idea how you felt about that subject or I would've explained myself better.'

'I think you were just letting your true colours show through.'

'If that's what you think then I can't do much about it.' He turned slightly in his chair, not so much that an observer would think he was snubbing her but the intention was clear. Lauren bit the inside of her lip. Was she being fair?

She tapped him on the shoulder and he turned back to look at her, his mouth still set in a firm line.

'If you promise me you'll keep an open mind about life in a country town, I'll let you off this once.' She smiled at him and it softened her words, letting him see she was making peace.

'Given that apologies aren't *your* style, Lauren Harrison, I'll accept that attempt at one.' He could see her hesitate for a second and then she smiled back at him. Her grin was wide and he'd missed it over the last few days. It was one in a million. He'd followed it to Port Cadney just like the sailors of old had orientated themselves by the North Star. Or maybe, like others, he'd been led astray by the songs of sirens. He'd better work out whether she was a star or siren before he ended up a wreck, too.

'What?'

He'd been staring while he'd been thinking and he'd been caught out. Not surprising. She had a mesmerising affect on people. He just hoped he hadn't been too obvious about his admiration. Even the irritation he'd felt at her over the last few days for being so damn bloody-minded when she got her teeth into an issue had vanished the second she'd smiled at him.

He shook his head. 'You don't want to know.'

'Sure I do. We're friends again, and friends talk.'

'Then as one friend to another, may I say you're looking stunning tonight.'

'Thank you. And I have to say leaving off the tie was a good touch. You're starting to blend in with the locals already. Can I offer you another tip to help your camouflage? You could lose the brand-new four-wheel-drive. You stick out a mile in that thing.'

He laughed. 'Give me a break, it's on loan.' How he loved it when she teased him. There were no games with her, she was direct and her zest for life blazed. 'What would you suggest I trade it in for anyway? A horse?'

'There you go again, stereotypes of country life rampaging through that city-bred head of yours. How about a four-wheel-drive that's actually been on a dirt road before, had a few miles put on it? Or are you afraid of getting your designer clothes dirty?' She flashed him a sweet smile.

'I've no objection to getting down and dirty, Lauren. You should at least remember that much about me.'

Lauren stifled the rush of heat that coursed through her but she could feel a blush creeping over her cheeks. Jack stood, smiling, one eyebrow cocked, suggesting something but she wasn't sure what. 'Will you excuse me for a minute?'

She watched him cross the dance floor to speak to the band leader. The flush in her cheeks subsided but she couldn't pretend she didn't enjoy watching him move.

He looked confident and relaxed. He didn't look like the new boy in town. Top to toe, the man was gorgeous.

He returned to her side. 'May I have the pleasure of this dance?'

She stood, taking his hand, and let him lead her onto the dance floor. When fast-paced Latin-American music started to play, her eyes opened wide with surprise. Jack slipped easily into the beat of the music and she followed, gasping when he brought her to stand against him, bodies close, holding her hand lightly in his and placing his arm around her back.

'You can actually dance. I thought you'd be all uptight and just wiggle from side to side.'

'Easy with the compliments.' He pulled her closer, guiding her with a firm hand in the middle of her back, their hips moving with the music as he led her in a succession of quick steps, twirling her out from him and back, then both turning together.

'Now I'm really impressed. What's this we're doing?'

'The merengue. There are lots of possible steps but the great thing is you only need the simplest few to be able to start. Like this.' He moved his feet backward, one after the other, and brought her with him, their knees coming together with each forward-back movement. 'Then you can add in other moves when you want. It's not like doing the foxtrot or—' she could see he was struggling to think of another dance '—the polka, where you have to do the steps the same way each time.'

Lauren was spluttering with laughter. 'The polka! Where on earth did you drag that thought up from? That can't have been heard of for at least twenty years.'

He joined in her laughter. 'I didn't say I did it, just that *this* isn't like it.'

'It certainly is not. My grandma would have a fit if

she saw this. She'd think it was like having sex in
public.'

'It *is* a sensual dance.' Jack spun her out and away
from him and Lauren continued the turn. 'I knew you'd
do that,' he said.

'Do what?'

'Lead. I wondered how long it'd be before you thought
you knew how to do this and take over.' He was laughing
at her and she started to protest but he talked over her.
'Feel the lead from my hands. See how I'm holding your
right hand, not too tight but not too loose? Feel it, you'll
feel from how I change my hold and the direction I turn
you in what we're doing. For once in your life, sit back
and enjoy the ride.'

'Humph.'

'Very mature, Lauren. It won't kill you, I promise. You
may actually start to enjoy it.'

'I think it's gone to your head that you're nimble on
the dance floor.'

It was Jack's turn to splutter with laughter. 'Nimble?
Lauren, I can tell you, if you ever want to make a man
feel unmanly, call him nimble.'

A second number started and this was even more up-
tempo. 'OK, Mr Nimble, show us what you can do. I
won't even lead.'

It was impossible for two people to dance any closer
together than they were. With her heels on, they were
almost the same height, and because they were so close
together, the only place she could look was straight into
his gorgeous eyes. She could feel his breath soft against
her cheek and she felt like taking great deep breaths of
the smell of him, wood and heat and spices. So what if
she was enjoying it? She'd feel the same thrill dancing
with any man who was so skilful on the dance floor, so

in tune with the rhythm that he could move his hips and his body so fluidly and look so masculine at the same time.

'Time for a break?'

She nodded. 'It's getting rather warm in here,' she said, then mentally kicked herself. It sounded like a pick-up line.

'I'll get us some drinks and I'll meet you outside.'

She nodded again. After all, they were work colleagues, nothing more. She'd go outside with any workmate. She headed for the exit but stopped in her tracks when a scream ripped through the air. She whipped around and saw Jack had turned, too, before they both headed straight in the direction of the noise.

A huddle of people were standing around a middle-aged man who'd collapsed on the floor, a woman kneeling at his side, screaming, 'Lenny, Lenny.'

Within seconds, Jack had the scene organised, reaching into his pocket and tossing Lauren his car keys. 'Get my bag from the car. It's just outside to the left.' Then he directed a nearby club member to order an ambulance.

He crouched next to the man, who appeared only semi-conscious, and said to the woman, 'I'm a doctor. Can you tell me what happened?'

'I'm Cassie. This is my husband, Lenny. He's been stumbling a bit tonight, he dropped a glass a few minutes ago. I thought maybe he'd had too much to drink, he's had a virus and has been very tired lately, but then he sort of just went down on the floor.' She looked up at Jack, and he could see how stricken she was, her mouth drawn up tight. 'Has he had a stroke?'

A heart attack was more likely but it was still too early to say for sure, too early to start suggesting causes to the man's panicked wife. He took Lenny's pulse. It was too high, 120 beats a minute, and his breathing was rapid.

'Does he have a heart condition? Any other medical condition? Diabetes or high blood pressure? Severe allergies?' He was hypothesis-testing as fast as he could. He hoped Lenny's wife had the information he needed to help him make an accurate diagnosis so he could decide on an action plan.

She shook her head. 'Just the virus this last week, and he's been feeling worse these last few days, much more tired.'

'Anything else?'

She gasped and Jack glanced at her, waiting for her to go on. 'He *did* go to our GP a few weeks ago and had a finger-prick test. She said his blood sugar was a bit high and told him he'd need more tests because he might have diabetes. Lenny ignored her, said he didn't feel sick so he didn't need a lot of doctors poking him with needles.'

Lenny was drifting further into unconsciousness. His eyelids were fluttering open less and less, and he was barely responding to Jack's attempts to rouse him by squeezing his shoulder or scraping his fingers over Lenny's palm.

'Has he been eating and drinking?' If he was right, there wasn't much he could do before the ambulance arrived but he needed to be sure.

She nodded. 'We both thought he couldn't be that sick if his appetite was so good.'

Lauren returned and crouched beside Jack, opening his bag and handing him a blood-pressure cuff when he asked.

'Heart rate?'

She placed her fingers over Lenny's carotid pulse and

started counting while Jack strapped the cuff around the patient's upper arm.

'One-twenty,' Lauren said.

Still too high. 'Take his temp.'

The blood pressure was no better. As he pulled the cuff off, he said to Lauren, 'BP 90 over 60.' He saw her slip the thermometer out of Lenny's mouth. 'What have you got?'

'Thirty-nine degrees.'

Lenny's heart rate and temperature were elevated and his systolic blood pressure was much too low. Jack had as much information as he could gather without additional equipment.

'Looks like we've got a non-ketotic hyperglycaemic coma on our hands.' He spoke quietly so Cassie couldn't hear. 'He needs fluids, fast.'

He knew he didn't need to spell it out to Lauren that, if his diagnosis was correct, Lenny would definitely slip into a coma without the fluids. He would be dangerously dehydrated and he was almost there already. 'Ambulance ETA?'

Jack saw Lauren look over her shoulder and blew out a breath of relief when he heard the words, 'They're here.'

As the two ambulance officers arrived, Jack wasted no time in bringing them up to date on Lenny's condition. 'Potential non-ketotic hyperglycaemic coma. He needs IV fluids and a blood-sugar check.'

One officer concentrated on inserting a giving set into Lenny's forearm to run the fluids while the other did a quick finger-prick test for blood-sugar levels, confirming that Lenny's BSLs were too high.

Jack nodded. 'That supports the diagnosis. I take it you won't administer insulin?'

'No, we'll leave that for the hospital, so they can monitor his BSLs properly.' He packed away the testing kit. 'We don't want to push him the other way.'

'Absolutely.' He'd been reluctant to question the officer, but he'd seen insulin administered inappropriately before. If they'd gone down that line, they would have run the risk of pushing Lenny into a hypoglycaemic coma because they couldn't monitor his BSLs as well as could be done in hospital.

Lauren took Cassie aside. She needed an explanation now, before she got to the hospital when things would be happening fast. 'It's most likely at this stage that your husband has had a hyperglycaemic episode. It's common in uncontrolled diabetes.'

'Will he be OK?'

'We need to get him to the hospital as soon as possible. The emergency staff there will be able to assess him and make sure he gets optimal treatment.'

'Is it because he's overweight?'

Lauren hesitated, then said, 'It could be a factor.'

'The silly old codger, I *told* him something like this would happen.' Cassie's nerves were stretched tight and Lauren knew she'd be in tears any minute.

Lenny had been transferred to the stretcher and the ambulance officers were pushing it towards the door.

Lauren put her arm around Cassie. 'You can go with him in the ambulance. I'll walk you out. Who is your family doctor?' Cassie named one of the local GPs Lauren knew well. 'I'll contact her and see if she can meet you at the hospital. I know she'd want to do that. For now, though, your husband will be in the hands of the emergency staff, OK?'

Cassie nodded and Lauren helped her into the back of

the ambulance where Lenny was already secured, one of the officers sitting by his side.

Lauren and Jack stepped out of the way as the officer who would be driving closed the back doors. They watched as he climbed behind the wheel and put the siren on, driving at speed out of the car park. The other guests who had followed the officers out went back inside, leaving Lauren and Jack alone.

'Are you sure of your diagnosis?'

'Almost certain.'

'What are his chances?'

'I think we got the fluids into him in time. But if we didn't his chances aren't so good. The death rate in this type of coma is about 40 per cent and there are multiple risks of complications like blood clots and cerebral oedemas,' he said, using the term for brain swelling.

'That's something that always blows me away. We always think we'll know when something bad is about to happen, but we don't.'

'It's human nature to think we control our lives much more than we do.' The lights in the car park illuminated them both and Jack watched the play of light across Lauren's face as he talked. 'I suppose it's much too terrifying to accept that there are many things we have no say in.' Like how I feel about you, he thought, but he didn't say it. He did still at least have control over his words. 'Then again, there were many things Lenny had control over, like his diet and exercise, which I would think were primary contributing factors to his collapse, or going for the recommended tests. And he still didn't do what was right for him.'

'I guess that means we're really all crazy at the end of the day, huh?'

'What I'm really crazy for right now…' he smiled and

took her hand in his, starting to walk towards the verandah where they'd been headed before Lenny's collapse
'…is that drink we were talking about.'

'Make mine a double.'

Jack raised an eyebrow but smiled when he realised
she was joking.

'You love riling me, don't you, Ms Harrison?'

'Absolutely.'

'I'm catching on, though, and one of these days I might
just turn the tables on you. Then what will you do?' He
winked at her and left her on the verandah, going inside
to get their drinks.

Lauren climbed onto the verandah railing and let her
legs swing back and forth as she looked out across the
tennis courts to the night sky, enjoying a few minutes'
solitude and letting the unpleasantness of Lenny's collapse wash away.

'The stars are incredible out here. It always surprises
me when I leave the city how stunning the night sky can
be.' Jack came to stand next to her, his shoulder touching
hers as he leant against the railing. She turned slightly to
take her glass.

'Where else have you been other than here?' It seemed
a perfect opportunity to turn the conversation to happier
topics.

'I've done a few months here and there in the country
during my training but I haven't been based in the outback for a number of years now.'

'Not your thing?'

He shrugged. 'It's not the direction I'm heading in.'

Lauren felt a warning flicker but ignored it. She'd
known all along that they wanted different things out
of life.

He continued, 'But it's given me some good memories along the way.'

'And taught you a thing or two about Latin-American dancing as well. Where did you learn that? It's not something I'd have associated with you.'

'I'll ignore that comment, it's about as flattering as calling me nimble.' He leant forward, resting his strong forearms on the railing, and Lauren felt a pull inside her, a yearning for him to move his hands to her legs, to feel his skin on hers.

She shook her head slightly to bring the image to an end and concentrate on what he was saying.

'I spent a few months in South America on my medical elective. It seems like a lifetime ago now.'

She shifted slightly, just enough to bring her leg in contact with his arm. 'Tell me about it.'

'It was fantastic. The people work hard and they play even harder. Even a quiet drink after work is more like an incredible party.'

'And the dancing?'

'There's nothing else like it. It's such a part of everyday life. The music starts and there's no way you can just sit down and watch. Even if you wanted to, there's immediately a host of people pulling you up to dance.'

Lauren felt an odd twist in her stomach at the thought of stunning Latin-American women dancing with Jack. Willing teachers wouldn't have been short on the ground for a man like him.

'And since you got home?'

'I've hung up my dancing shoes.'

'Why?'

'Too busy working.'

'I see.'

'What?'

'All work and no play makes Jack a dull boy.'

'These comments of yours are getting out of hand.' He placed a hand on her waist and pulled her around to face him fully. 'Was it because I'm so dull that you spent a month with me in Adelaide?'

He bent his head slightly and in a moment the teasing light in his eyes darkened to become something much more personal. He wanted her, she could see it.

'Was it this you found dull?'

She felt a tremor of expectation ripple through her as he raised his other hand to stroke the back of her neck.

He leant closer and pulled her in towards him so she was pressed against his broad chest before scooping her legs over the railing and bringing her to stand hard against him. It was so sudden she couldn't protest but she knew, deep down, that this was the reason she'd come outside.

The night air was still warm about them and it was mixed with the warmth from his body and his breath, soft on her face. She could feel herself melting into the spell of the night and this man, and she pushed other thoughts aside, wanting the moment to consume her and lift her beyond place and time.

He brushed a roughened thumb over her cheek, the contrast in textures almost causing her to purr like a kitten. She felt malleable beneath his touch. He bent his head closer to hers and said quietly, 'Or perhaps it was this.'

CHAPTER FOUR

JACK lowered his lips to Lauren's and the seconds stretched between them, both waiting to see what would happen, how she would react. She felt as though she were a spectator with no way of stopping events.

He spanned his fingers across the back of her neck before running them along her spine, his touch light enough to tease and deep enough to promise. He lowered his head closer still until his mouth was only a fraction away from hers, and she could feel his breath warm on her lips as he whispered, 'I don't think it could possibly be this, but we'll have to try it, just to make sure.' His voice was deep and soft and it washed over her, pulling her along with it, winding around her like a hypnotic dream.

Lauren lifted her face up just as Jack brought his lips down to hers and they met in a kiss that would be causing sleepless nights for at least one of them for days to come. It started slowly and, as the memory of other kisses came flooding back, she could feel them spilling into the moment. Lips against lips, tongues tasting, teasing. Lauren ran her fingers through Jack's short, thick hair and pulled his head down harder. This kiss couldn't lead to anything and the knowledge drove her to wring every last ounce of pleasure from it. She pressed her body against his and a tremor ran through her as she felt the hard shaft of his arousal against her. He deepened the kiss in response to her silent urging, his tongue flicking against hers. Slowly, she ran her hands from his neck down the length of his spine, spreading her fingers over his lower back, holding him against her, body to body.

He groaned and cupped her face between his large hands and she could feel the strength of him even though his touch was gentle. His mouth left her lips and he whispered her name and gathered her hair in one hand at the back of her head, twisting it and then letting it fall before running his fingers through its silky length. Her eyelids fluttered open and she felt a strange emotion rip through her as she saw the passion in his eyes. Somehow that was enough to warn her. If she didn't stop here she'd soon be unable to make that choice. She glanced beyond him, back in the direction they had come from, and stepped away, forcing him to take his hands from her hair. This had to end here. Lauren folded her arms across her chest in a protective gesture, putting some distance between them.

'This isn't fair, Jack. You can't come waltzing in here and disrupt things like this.' Maybe her words were harsh but she could hear the pleading in her voice. 'There's never been anything more than a casual fling between us and I can't do that here.'

'Why not?' he asked as he bent his head to kiss her again.

Lauren put up a hand to stop him. 'In a country town, no one's business is private. This is my home town, my life. Where on earth could anything between us go?'

'Why do we have to have it all worked out right now?'

She looked away but he put two fingers beneath her chin and tilted her head up gently, forcing her to meet his gaze. 'You don't really think it's over between us. The way you kissed me just now proves that.'

Lauren paused, she couldn't deny it. That kiss had been heaven. 'Why did you come here?'

'Work.'

'Is that all? It's quite a coincidence, don't you think, you landing here, in my home town?'

'Not as much of a coincidence as some might think. You're right, knowing you were still here was the deciding factor.'

'And you think that's fair?'

'You keep saying that. What's fair got to do with it?'

'A lot when it's my life you're messing with.'

'What are you afraid of?'

'We're going around in circles. We're two very different people and we're going different places. Just because we had great sex doesn't mean there's anything more to it.'

There was a twinkle back in his eyes. 'Glad to hear you agree about the sex at least. What was it, do you think? Is it because I'm nimble in the bedroom?'

She stifled a laugh. He could win her over every time. It didn't get more dangerous than that.

'We both know that this attraction is not going to disappear just because you want it to. It's been six months and it hasn't diminished at all.'

'Six months and five days,' Lauren muttered. Her heart ached with desire and regret.

'You might think you've got me out of your system but I beg to differ.'

'It doesn't matter anyway. We work together and that's all.' She tried to sound decisive as she turned to walk away. But all she felt was disappointment as Jack let her go.

The following morning Lauren raced out the door, cursing for having slept in on her day off. Half a dozen things on her 'to do' list remained undone plus, if she didn't hurry, she'd be late for her teenage mothers' social meeting. Running to her car port, a familiar voice stopped her in her tracks.

'Where's the fire?'

'Jack! What are you doing here?'

'Chloe set up an appointment for me to have a look at unit three. I've just finished. Where are you off to?'

'My mothers' group starts in—' Lauren glanced at her watch '—seven and a half minutes.'

'Mothers' group?'

'The group for teenage mothers that I told you about.'

'Hmm.'

She took one look at Jack's expression. 'Don't start. I'm running late as it is and I don't have time to argue.'

'Why don't I drop you off? Then we can argue on the way.' Jack was laughing.

The minute he laughed Lauren forgot about being late. His eyes sparkled and his full lips parted to show even white teeth. All arguments against him flew out the window when he looked at her that way. Somehow her brain short-circuited and only her heart responded.

'Where do you have to go?'

'The community health centre, next door to the hospital.'

'Right. Let's go.'

Remembering Ryan's earlier suggestion, she said, 'If you're not busy, maybe you should come to the meeting and see what it's all about. Maybe one day soon I'll even manage to persuade you to give a talk on first aid for neonates. I seem to remember that it's a special interest of yours.'

Jack's glance showed Lauren that he hadn't forgotten how they'd first met.

'Who have you had as speakers before?'

'Sarah Fitzpatrick has done lectures on exercise, Joan, the lactation consultant, has also visited and Matt does an immunisation information morning.'

'Sarah Fitzpatrick?'

'She's a physio at the hospital—she's Ryan's sister-in-law.'

'And all this is done in their own time.'

Lauren hesitated. 'Not all of it.'

'So who pays for it?'

'The allied health practitioners schedule it into their day so their salaries cover it. They have blocks of time allocated for education and training, and postnatal groups meet the criteria for this. Matt usually comes in on his time off.'

'What about you?'

'Mostly I try to schedule the meetings on my rostered days off but sometimes they're on an on-call day.'

'So you don't get paid?'

'No. But I told you I think it's a worthwhile thing to be doing. I don't do it for financial reward.' Lauren indicated to Jack where he should park the car.

'What's on today's agenda?' They climbed out of the car and started walking towards the low brick building.

'Marilyn, the dietician, is coming to talk about introducing solids. Some of the babies are getting close to four months old now.' Lauren pushed open the door to the lecture room and got busy greeting the mums. There was one new mum today and the babies ranged in age from six weeks to four months. Marilyn was due to arrive in fifteen minutes, which gave the five mums time for a cup of tea and a chat first.

Lauren introduced herself to the new recruit first, then moved around the room, catching up with each girl and, by way of a friendly chat, listening carefully to see if anyone seemed to be having problems. Jack stood at the back of the room and watched Lauren as she chatted, held babies and made tea. She gave each girl her undivided attention which meant that Jack was free to observe her. She had so much energy about her. On anyone else her gestures would have looked exaggerated but on Lauren they just served to reinforce her passion for everything around her. Even her laugh had the full force of her personality behind it.

She turned and caught Jack's eye, motioning for him to join her. She raised her voice to the group. 'This is Jack Montgomery. He's our newest flying doctor. I persuaded him to come today so he can see what we do. I'm hoping to convince him to be a guest speaker for us.' The mothers nodded to Jack then went back to their babies and cups of tea.

All Jack could see was children nursing children. A huge responsibility to have at their age but he was impressed with their commitment to their babies. Coming here today showed they were keen to do their best as parents.

'Marilyn, hello.' Jack heard Lauren's greeting and turned to see a short, trim woman in her forties approaching.

Lauren clapped her hands for quiet. 'OK, everyone, this is Marilyn. As you know, she's a dietician but to answer Janet's question from last time—no, Marilyn is not here to tell you new mums how to lose those last stubborn kilograms. She's going to talk to us about introducing solids into your babies' diets.' Lauren's introduction drew a laugh from the girls before everyone settled back into the easy chairs and prepared to listen.

Marilyn gave an informative talk, covering how to introduce solid foods, which ones to start with, what consistency and how quickly to introduce new foods. She discussed the importance of giving finger foods as the babies developed and which foods were suitable for that.

At the conclusion of Marilyn's talk Lauren stood and thanked her before saying, 'I'm sure there are some questions if you've got time.'

Chrissy, nursing her three-month-old daughter, got the ball rolling. 'My sister's baby had a bad allergy to peanut butter. Should I let Louise have peanut butter or not?'

'Some allergies do seem to run in families and allergies to nuts and eggs seem to be becoming more common. If you've got a family history of allergies I would delay introducing those foods until after two years of age, particularly with any nut products. There's no need for children to eat peanut butter so, to answer your question, keep Louise off peanut butter until she's two.'

'What about eggs? They're a bit more important, aren't they?' Sharon's mum asked.

'Start with hard-boiled egg yolks, it's the white that's usually the cause of any problems. Mix the yolk in with some mashed vegetables and only start with a small portion, say a quarter of a yolk. But don't introduce the yolk until your baby is six months of age. I've got a leaflet for each of you outlining what I've covered here today, and it includes information on eggs. There are also some really easy, nutritious recipes to try. Babies have quite adventurous tastes so don't be afraid to give them lots of different things to try. It's not until they're about two that they start to become a bit fussy. That's when you'll find they want to eat the same thing every night.'

The questions came thick and fast and ranged from the right time to wean to how to sterilise bottles and how to get sufficient iron into a baby's diet.

Finally it was over and Jack waited as Lauren said her

goodbyes and confirmed the date of the next meeting. Together they walked back to the car. 'So how do you think it went?'

'The level of interaction was terrific.'

'They're good mums. Just because they're young doesn't make them stupid.'

'I wasn't implying that. I've given plenty of talks to know that just because I'm interested in a subject doesn't mean my audience is. But to hear them asking relevant questions was great. I'm sure Marilyn was pleased with their response.' Jack stopped walking and turned to Lauren. 'Tell me why you run these classes out of the goodness of your heart.'

'The community health service already runs postnatal classes but they didn't have enough nurses to run a new one specifically for teenage mums. It was my idea, and something I feel really strongly about, so I offered to get them up and running.'

'But why *do* they need their own sessions? Can't they join in with the others?' Surely Lauren's sessions were doubling up on a community service already in place? He didn't want to prejudge but that was a particular bugbear of his. Inefficiencies always rubbed him up the wrong way.

'Often they feel like the odd ones out. They respond really well in these sessions because no one is casting any blame or aspersions on them or their characters. Some feel the community is judging them and it's good for them to be able to get away from that scrutiny.'

He nodded, surprised, because what she was saying actually did make sense.

'Now that you've seen a session, do you think I could persuade you to talk to them about neonatal first aid?'

'I think you could persuade me to do just about anything.' He caught her hand in his and the way the simple contact made his heart race underscored the truth of his statement. 'Why don't you have dinner with me tonight and we can talk about it then?'

CHAPTER FIVE

'TELL me,' she said, changing the subject. 'What did you think of the unit?'

The corners of Jack's mouth twitched like he knew she'd deliberately stalled on his dinner invitation. 'The unit was nice enough but I really needed something that was furnished.'

'Why?' Lauren paused but then continued on, realising the answer to her question. 'Because you're not planning on staying and you don't want to move your things here just for a short while.'

Jack's silence confirmed her suspicions. Just as she'd thought—he was using his time and experience here as a stepping stone to bigger things. Part of a grand plan, a means to an end, rather than the end.

She took a deep breath. 'I don't think dinner is a good idea. There's no point in us starting something that can go nowhere. You don't plan on staying and I don't plan on leaving.'

'That didn't seem to bother you in Adelaide.'

'Things aren't the same here. Our time in Adelaide was just a bit of fun. Things are different in a small town.'

'This could be fun, too.' Jack's voice dropped in tone, whispering to Lauren, calling her to him.

'I'm not looking for fun.'

'Is there someone else?'

The moment Jack said the words the realisation hit her like a physical blow. In her mind there wasn't anyone else. She'd known that for a long time and had seen that clearly for the first time last night. But there was someone she needed to talk to. Although he had no claim on her now, she couldn't do anything with a clear conscience until she'd spoken to Ryan. Not that she was going to do anything.

She held her hand up to shield her eyes against the glare of the early afternoon sun as she looked up at him. 'Would you excuse me? I have mountains of errands today.'

He hesitated, wondering how he could stop her from leaving. 'Coffee first?'

She shook her head. 'I've got to go.'

Lauren's eyes snapped open. She shot a glance at her alarm clock, reaching out to shut it off before she registered the time. Two a.m. The noise wasn't her alarm. Gratefully she closed her eyes again. She'd taken ages to get to sleep, her chat with Ryan had kept replaying in her head.

That noise again. Her mobile phone. She sat up and grabbed it.

'Hello.'

'Lauren, it's Sheila. We've got a woman with abdominal pain. I need you for a flight.'

'See you in five.' Lauren was already out of bed, pulling on her uniform, by the time Sheila had disconnected the call. Ten minutes later she was sipping a coffee, waiting as Steve made the final checks to the aircraft. It was a beautiful, clear night and millions of stars shone in the sky. The Southern Cross was so bright it looked as if she could reach up and touch it. Steve called to her, interrupting her stargazing, and she climbed into the plane, taking the copilot's seat. She flipped through her medical notes, refreshing her memory on various abdominal complaints and their signs and symptoms as Steve guided the plane through the night.

The airstrip on the station came into sight. Someone had lined the strip with flares and they were burning brightly, illuminating the ground. The smoke drifting across the strip indicated the wind direction. The landing was smooth and Lauren unbuckled her seat belt and gathered her kit.

Her patient, Jenny Clarke, was the station's cook. Lauren examined her as she lay on her bed. Jenny was a middle-aged, overweight lady with an old appendectomy scar.

'I don't think it's appendicitis, Jenny,' Lauren said with confidence.

'But I've had this exact pain before. I remember it.'

'I'm sure you do.' She smothered a smile. 'But I'm also sure you've already had your appendix removed and I've never known one to grow back. Where exactly is the pain?' Jenny indicated the right upper abdominal quadrant. Too high for appendicitis. 'When did it start?' Lauren asked.

'About an hour after dinner. I thought it was indigestion at first.' Jenny cried out with pain, grabbing her right shoulder.

'Where was that pain?'

'In my shoulder blade.'

Jenny's breathing was rapid and shallow. Lauren gently palpated Jenny's abdomen, watching her patient's face closely for signs of distress. 'I think I'm going to be sick.'

Lauren leapt up to grab a bowl but wasn't quick enough. Jenny vomited over the floor, narrowly missing Lauren's shoes.

When Jenny had stopped, Lauren wiped her face and

neck with a damp towel before passing her a small glass of water. 'I'm pretty sure the pain is due to gallstones. I'll give you something for the pain but you'll need to fly back with us to be checked out.'

Jenny was in no condition to argue. She lay back on the bed and nodded in agreement.

Lauren settled Jenny, buckled onto a stretcher, into the plane. Satisfied that the painkillers were working, she left her for a few moments to place a call to the base.

Lauren walked beside the stretcher as Connor wheeled Jenny into the District Hospital. Jenny was whisked straight to Radiology and Lauren sat down to wait. She'd offered to assist in Theatre, if necessary. It saved waking someone else up in the early hours of the morning, and she was certain her diagnosis was accurate and she'd be needed. Lauren lay on the couch in the staffroom. A quick twenty-minute nap would get her through the next few hours.

'Good call.'

Lauren sat bolt upright on the couch. Jack was standing in front of her, holding an ultrasound film. His hair was damp, as if he'd quickly wet it down to combat tousled hair, and the shadow of his beard darkened his jaw. Even at five in the morning, dressed in operating scrubs, he looked delicious.

'I was right?'

'Right as rain. Two rather spectacular gallstones. Jenny is being prepped for Theatre as we speak.'

Lauren smiled. She hadn't doubted that Jenny had needed to come to town but it was always nice to have a diagnosis confirmed. Her smile turned into a yawn.

Jack saw. 'Are you sure you're OK to assist? You're not too tired?'

'I'm fine. I could do this in my sleep.'

'I'd rather you didn't if it's all the same to you.' Jack's eyes crinkled, his sense of humour easing what could have been an awkward moment.

Lauren hadn't wanted to think about their next meeting since she'd run off yesterday, straight to Ryan. This was probably best, meeting unexpectedly in a work situation. It meant they just had to get on with things. It didn't delay the inevitable but it did ease some tension.

'I'll get changed.' Lauren stood before Jack had a chance to move back. He was closer to the couch than she'd thought and she found herself standing almost chest to chest with him. She breathed in, his unique scent bombarding her senses, making her heart race. She felt her cheeks start to burn and rather than look at him she cast her eyes down to the floor just as he stepped back. She'd pushed him away yesterday, told him nothing could happen between them, but her face must be making a liar of her. She raced to the change rooms to compose herself before scrubbing for Theatre.

The anonymity of the face masks, caps and gowns in Theatre gave her some respite. She could almost pretend that the operating surgeon was anyone, or no one. Almost.

Jack was nothing if not professional and to anyone else all would have appeared normal. But for her, standing at his left shoulder, passing instruments and holding tools, their arms brushing against each other, it was torture. Sweet, tantalising torture. To be so near, to be able to feel his body heat through the thin cotton of the theatre gowns and yet not be able to touch him, was agonising. His effect on her made her options clear. She either had to keep her distance or fall under his spell. Again.

The laparoscopy was straightforward. A small incision into Jenny's gallbladder and Jack swiftly removed the two offending calcium deposits and dropped them into a kidney dish.

Thirty minutes from start to finish and Lauren was free. Until the next time. They had to talk, she knew that. She couldn't delay the inevitable for ever. But for now she was safe. She knew that Jack would wait to make sure there were no immediate post-op complications and this gave her some time. Time to shower, have breakfast and get back to the AAS base, ready for another day.

Her respite was short-lived.

'Good morning again.' Jack had come into the staff kitchen behind her. 'Thanks for your help in Theatre. It was good work.'

'How is Jenny?'

'Resting comfortably. She shouldn't have any problems as long as she watches her diet.' Jack looked as if he was about to say something more but changed his mind. 'Can I make you a coffee?'

She nodded, watching as Jack poured milk into two mugs and put them in the microwave to heat. What was she going to say to him? She'd hardly stopped thinking about the situation since she'd seen Ryan yesterday, but she was no closer to deciding what to actually do. Just when she'd decided to tell Jack there couldn't be anything between them, her libido would kick in and she'd change her mind. It was at those times that a voice in her head would taunt her with the question, What harm could another quick fling do?

The microwave pinged and Jack took the mugs out and filled them up with coffee from the filter pot, turning to pass one to her. Their fingers brushed as he handed it over and she managed not to jump with the flash of energy that zipped between them with the contact. The spark that had brought them together in Adelaide hadn't diminished, that much was certain.

Jack sat down opposite her and wrapped his hands around his mug. Silence fell but it was a companionable sort of silence, each of them busy with their thoughts.

Lauren sipped at her coffee and crunched a chocolate biscuit. Every now and then she braved a look across at Jack, and although she was sure he knew she was doing it, he kept his head bent to the medical journal he'd now opened before him. Maybe now was the opportunity she needed, her chance to set things straight. Who knew when she'd get another chance?

She swallowed the last bit of biscuit and drained her coffee, putting the mug on the table just as Ryan and Steve walked in and the opportunity was gone. Thank goodness Steve was there, too. The old saying 'Two's company, three's a crowd' sprang to mind. She'd have felt terribly self-conscious if it hadn't been for Steve's presence.

She needn't have worried. Ryan seemed completely unfazed, nodding a greeting to them both and heading for the kettle. Had she expected him to challenge Jack to a duel, pistols at dawn? It wasn't his style, she knew that. His reaction to her news last night was proof of that. But still, she'd expected some awkwardness between them.

Ryan, in his typical, laid-back, country male way, had taken her decision almost without comment. They'd shared a beer, two old friends catching up, discussing the latest news. Except the latest news had been Jack Montgomery. She'd left wondering why she'd waited so long to say anything. He'd hardly been devastated. He would've been more upset if something had happened to his beloved Border collie.

She looked into her coffee cup and thought about Ryan's reaction. He'd guessed that Jack's arrival had thrown her into a spin but thankfully he didn't seem to know about the kiss at the country club. One comment he'd made stayed with her—she wasn't sure if it had been directed at her or himself—'Sometimes what we want isn't the way things work out.'

She needed to talk to Jack, and soon. And it couldn't be soon enough to put an end to the emotional merry-go-round she'd been on ever since he'd walked back into her life.

Sheila poked her head around the door. 'Sorry to interrupt your break but a call's just come through for an early delivery. Julie and Tony Masters, one-hour flight. Tony says there were some concerns last week that the baby was breech. Contractions six minutes apart and progressing quickly by the sound of things.'

Steve, Jack and Lauren were on their feet and heading out to the plane as Sheila finished speaking. Without discussing it, Jack and Lauren had known they'd both need to attend this one. They worked well together. It was a pity this attraction had complicated the work situation. And then, of course, there was that other matter, the fact that he'd be off again in a couple of months or so anyway.

Lauren motioned for Jack to join her and Steve up front as soon as they were safely airborne.

'I've got Tony Masters here.'

Jack slipped the headphones over his ears, and after brief introductions got down to business, gathering information about Julie's contractions and pain levels and giving the worried father-to-be some instructions, before passing over to Lauren.

She spoke with Tony for a few minutes, talking him through his anxiety and adding a few suggestions of her own to help him with his wife. She ended the call and took off her headphones.

'Some of those ideas sounded a little unorthodox,' said Jack, amusement shining in his eyes.

She laughed. 'I thought it would keep him busy. Otherwise he's bound to have her stress levels sky-high before we get there by worrying over her. We're still half an hour away.' She tapped Steve on the shoulder. 'Let me know when we're nearly there. We'll just go and run through the situation.'

Steve nodded and Lauren and Jack went back to the cabin to the same places they'd sat on Jack's first day. It was the perfect opportunity to straighten a few things out, if she could only stick with one decision for more than a few minutes at a time.

Jack leant across the aisle towards her, raising his fingers to her face and brushing them lightly across her skin. 'You've got biscuit crumbs on your cheek.'

'All gone?'

He nodded.

She watched him while he sat across the aisle from her. Jack was intelligent, confident and the sexiest man she'd ever laid eyes on. He made her feel alive in a way that no other man ever had. And no one else had ever pushed all her buttons like he did either. She was starting to feel like she was on a sensory roller-coaster, going from infatuated to infuriated in the space of a few seconds. Her senses were heightened when he was around. She knew that if she closed her eyes she'd still be able to feel his presence. Maybe it was the strength of his personality, his force, that she could feel. Her dad had always said she needed someone she couldn't push around, and she recognised Jack's determination. She saw the same thing in herself. An equal, her dad had said. She tapped her fingers on her thighs, drumming a mindless rhythm. Maybe there was something in her dad's view. But, at the end of the day, Jack was a city boy. So he couldn't be the one for her.

She knew that for sure.

At least, she thought she did.

Brief affair or not, Jack could never be any more than a fling, and her physical attraction to him was so great there was a risk she'd throw aside her dreams just to be with him. Falling in love with him could only take her one place—away from the country and her plans. It was a no-go situation and she wasn't going to risk it. The best idea she'd had was to have a final fling with him—maybe that would get him out of her system. But what if it didn't?

'Let's get you into position, then we can have a look and see how you and baby are going.' They'd arrived to find Julie only marginally more distressed than her husband.

'I want you to take me to town. I don't want a home birth.'

'Let's have a look at you and then we'll have a talk.' Jack's voice was calm and Julie responded, a little less panicked now that at least the medics had arrived.

Lauren and Jack both scrubbed for the examination then Lauren manoeuvred Julie back on the bed, propping her up on a mound of pillows that she'd got Tony to gather before they'd arrived.

Julie was hit by another contraction and grabbed Lauren by the arm as she was settling her on the pillows.

She was gritting her teeth, tensed up, and Lauren talked to her gently, rubbing her lower back. 'Easy there, Julie, remember your breathing. Nice and slow, breathe through it.' She soothed her for the duration of the contraction, then said, 'Let's have a look at you now, see how you're doing.'

Lauren motioned Tony to come and stand next to his wife while Jack checked Julie's dilatation. She talked to Tony to keep his mind on helping his wife. 'Did you see what I was doing with Julie then?' A pale Tony nodded. 'When the next contraction hits, I want you to do the same thing, talk her through her breathing and rub her back.'

Jack looked up at Lauren. 'Six centimetres.'

Lauren nodded and set about taking base-line observations. She slipped a thermometer under Julie's tongue and took her blood pressure, writing down both results before taking Julie's pulse.

'You're doing well,' was all she had time to tell her before another contraction hit Julie hard. Lauren automatically glanced at her watch, passing the timing on to Jack. 'Three minutes apart.' Neither of them needed to say the words. With a one-hour flight ahead of them and a possible breech birth, this was one labour that was going to happen at home. And soon.

'Monitor, please.'

Lauren took the foetal heart-rate monitor from the bag and positioned it around Julie's abdomen. The readout indicated that, so far at least, the baby's heart rate was normal. Lauren watched Jack as he continued his examination. She could see the tiny muscles in his jaw tense, but to everyone else he appeared relaxed and in control. Always in control.

'Baby's coming quickly but the good news is, if he

was breech, he's now turned himself around. He's facing the wrong way, forwards instead of backwards, but that's no drama—just means a bit more discomfort for you.'

'It can't get much worse than this,' Julie muttered between clenched teeth as another contraction hit.

Lauren felt her own heart pick up pace as she waited. The foetal heart monitor was still attached and she kept an eye on the readout while taking repeat observations on Julie. So far so good, despite Julie becoming increasingly anxious. Tony, meanwhile, was looking greener by the second and Lauren decided he'd be more use out of the room for a while.

'Is there any music Julie wanted to have playing at the birth? Special candles, things like that?' She'd mentioned this to him during the flight but he clearly hadn't retained much of that conversation. He looked nonplussed for a moment before latching on to the idea that Lauren was offering him a moment of escape. She could see his train of thought as clearly as if it were painted on his face, and if the situation hadn't been so intense, she'd have allowed herself a silent chuckle.

'I'll be right back, sweetheart,' he said to his wife.

'You'd better be,' muttered Julie between clenched teeth as another contraction hit. 'I'm going to hold your hand so tight it breaks.'

Julie's contractions were coming one minute apart now and Jack repeated his examination. He nodded to Lauren and she went to call Tony.

As she returned to the room Jack was saying, 'OK, Julie, when the next contraction hits I want you to push. Can you do that?'

'I want Tony.'

'He's coming.'

'I'm going to kill him. This is all your fault, Tony.'

Tony appeared, looking distraught, and Lauren reassured him that women in labour threatened all sorts of violence towards their husbands and then promptly forgot about it once the baby was born. He looked only slightly less terrified.

'Right, get ready, Julie.'

'I can't do this. I don't want a baby.'

'It's all right, Julie, you're doing well.' Lauren watched as Jack checked the position of the umbilical cord. 'Push now, a nice long push until I tell you to stop. That's it, keep going.' Jack talked her through the contraction. 'Terrific, I can see his head. Have a rest now. OK, with the next contraction you can push his head out and then you're nearly done. Ready, go.'

The baby's head crowned and with the next contraction the baby surged out and Jack just managed to catch the slippery little body.

'Congratulations, Mum and Dad, you have a beautiful baby boy. You've done well, Mum, very well.' Jack's voice was full of pride for the new parents, genuine delight, as if this was the first baby he'd ever helped into the world.

Lauren swallowed a lump in her throat. Births always made her gooey, and seeing Jack moved too added to the moment.

She took the baby and started to record his Apgar scores while Jack gave Julie an injection of oxytocin to assist delivery of the placenta. She smiled at the little boy, screaming and wriggling in her hands. 'Nothing wrong with your lungs, little man.' She wrapped the baby and placed him at Julie's breast, then looked at Tony, wanting to see his reaction to her next question. 'Do you want to cut the cord, Dad?'

Tony turned a shade paler and sat down on the bed next to his wife. 'Go on,' Julie urged him.

'It's OK, Tony, you don't get extra points for doing it. But if you'd like to have a go, it's pretty straightforward.'

'I won't hurt the baby?'

'Absolutely not.'

The cord had stopped pulsating so Jack clamped it. With reluctance Tony came forward, but at the sight of his son he seemed to find a new source of courage, taking the scissors and cutting the cord.

'Everything's fine, he's a beautiful healthy baby.' Lauren directed her next words to Julie. 'It's nice and warm in here, so unwrap him and hold him against your skin, get to know him. Do you have a name for him?'

Lauren watched as Julie, wonder shining on her face, held the blanket back from her baby's face.

'Cooper. His name is Cooper.'

Jack glanced at Lauren, and she nodded and said, 'We'll leave you all alone now, and come back in a while to check on things. Shout if you need us.'

As they left the room, they heard Tony saying in a voice laden with pride, 'I don't reckon there was ever a woman who did as well as you just now. I'm chuffed, Jules, you've made me the happiest man in the world.'

Lauren couldn't resist a final peek over her shoulder. Baby Cooper was nestled in the arms of his teary mother, who was lying in her husband's embrace. She wasn't sure, but she thought she heard Julie whisper in an awe-inspired voice, 'We're a family.'

There was an extra spring in her step as they went in search of Steve, who she'd guessed would have made himself comfortable somewhere near a kettle. They smelt the fresh tea before they saw him, stretched out in a kitchen chair.

'All's well?'

'Thanks to our own Boy Wonder, yes, it is.' Lauren waved an arm in Jack's direction, giving credit where it was due.

'Glad to hear it. Want a cup?'

Lauren chuckled and nodded. Steve was the opposite of Ryan, who was always genuinely interested in how things had gone and what had happened. If ever Steve's help was needed, he was more than happy to oblige but voluntarily engaging in post-partum discussions was not his idea of fun. 'Could you make an extra two cups—'

'With lots of sugar? Sure. There are sandwiches, too.' He nodded at an enormous pile of thick-cut slices of bread filled with ham and mustard. 'There should even be enough to keep you happy.'

Lauren grabbed a sandwich and started to munch, taking big gulps of hot sweet tea between bites. She was aware of Jack looking in her direction but it didn't make her unsettled. Instead, it added to the warm glow that suffused her, on a high after the birth. All was right with the world.

'What are the chances of leaving now?' Jack asked.

'We can't. The strip isn't nearly well lit enough and it's late, too dark to leave.'

Lauren stood up and stretched her arms over her head before sweeping them down towards the floor and letting them hang there for a few seconds, getting her blood flowing and clearing her head before righting herself again. 'I'll go see to them and explain the situation and you guys report back to base.' She took a tray from the kitchen dresser and piled fresh cups of tea and plates of sandwiches onto it.

Lauren knocked at the door. 'Sustenance, anyone?'

She could see Julie hesitate and glance at her son so she offered, 'How about I take him while you recharge your batteries?'

It was the permission Julie needed to hand over the baby. 'How about you—' she nodded at Tony '—have something to eat and drink, too, then you can help me get everything ready for his first wash?'

'Sure,' said Tony. 'After the labour, a bath should be a piece of cake.'

Two hours later, the newly formed family unit was settled in bed for their first night together. Lauren had shown Julie how to help Cooper attach for breast-feeding and so far all was going well. The AAS staff would be staying in the shearers' quarters for the night and the new parents would ring Lauren's mobile if they needed anything.

Lauren and Jack made one last check on mother and son. Satisfied that everything was fine, they left the main house and walked in silence across the yard towards their quarters. The coolness of the dark night contrasted with the warmth of the day and the house. Jack still wasn't used to how cold the nights were in comparison to the day's heat.

He opened the front door and they walked straight into a large sitting room, complete with small kitchen. Six doors, open to show a bathroom and bedrooms, opened off the main room. One door was closed and they could hear a muffled snoring sound from behind it.

'Nice of Steve to provide us with a bit of mood music,' said Jack as he prowled around the room, opening cupboards and making himself at home.

'Is that what you call it? Then you can have the room next to him. I'm sleeping as far away as I can get.' She followed his lead and opened the fridge, reaching inside for a bottle of white wine, which had a note attached.

'Look what Tony left us.' She turned over the card and read out his thanks. 'Isn't that lovely? He must have torn himself away from his son to do it.' She put it down on the counter and rummaged about for a corkscrew. 'Feel like a glass?'

'We're still on duty.'

'No, we're not really and, anyway, we're entitled to have a break. I'm not talking about getting plastered, just having a glass.'

Jack shook his head. 'You're determined to corrupt me.'

'Absolutely.' She pulled the cork on the bottle of wine. 'Will you put up much of a fight?'

'I'm afraid I'm putty in your hands,' he replied as she poured the wine.

Lauren carried their glasses to an old couch that had seen better days. Jack took his glass and they sat down, Lauren curling up with one leg under her, her stomach doing strange twists at the thought of Jack being anything at all in her hands. Mmm. Delicious.

'Lauren, there *is* something I need to know. I like to play by the rules so I need to know what they are.' He had his 'serious business' expression on. 'Are you involved with anyone else?'

She shook her head.

'In that case—' he leant towards her and clinked his glass against hers '—here's to us.'

Lauren raised her face to meet his dark eyes, serious still but no longer concerned, just intent. His message was clear. He wanted her and he wanted her to know it. And she did. But where did that leave her intention to sort things out with him?

He smiled. A gorgeous smile that made her feel she was the only woman who'd ever seen it. A smile that made her long to throw caution to the winds and lose herself in his embrace. She took a gulp of wine to steady her nerves and tried to remember what her decision had been.

'I was going to tell you that there can be no ''us'' but when you smile at me, I have to admit, my head seems to switch off.'

'Excellent. Keep it that way and come over here.' He held his arms open to her.

She raised an eyebrow, not quite ready to give up her resolutions. 'For someone who thought he couldn't have a drink on duty, you seem very happy to indulge in other areas.'

He laughed, the sound deep and rich and lovely. 'Entirely different things. Kissing you senseless won't affect my ability to deal with a problem in the middle of the night. Polishing off half a bottle of wine, on the other hand…'

'What a cheek. As if kissing me wouldn't leave you stunned with passion for the next few hours.' She was only half joking. The thought of it was certainly knocking her sideways.

He leant forward, catching her wrists in his large hands and encircling them with his fingers. Hot ripples ran through her and her vision wavered for a second until all at once they were kissing. She wasn't sure who had leant forward first, it had just happened.

He laid her down against the seat, still gently holding her wrists crossed against her chest, and the urge to draw her hands away and run them over him did battle with the thrill of letting him take control. It was deliciously frustrating to want to pull him down harder but not being able to. She knew he could sense her excitement but also that she was safe with him. She trusted him. Trusting herself was another matter.

His kisses were almost unbearably gorgeous, teasing her with the promise that soon he'd kiss her more deeply, but for now was holding himself in check, touching his lips against hers, exploring, tasting, still under control. He lifted his mouth from hers and she felt the loss of it, flickering open her eyes to protest until she realised he was kissing maddening little trails down her neck, towards the open neck of her shirt. It was as if they were in Adelaide again, in their mad and wonderful month together, when every spare moment had been spent exploring and worshipping each other's bodies. Whatever happened tomorrow, however long he was going to stay, the only thing that mattered right now was being with Jack, feeling his arms around her, enfolding the two of them in their own private world. The feelings she'd thought she'd buried were still there, as intense as they'd been all those months ago. The memory of the pain she'd felt after they'd parted was suddenly dim by comparison. Only the magic of his touch, the taste of him, the feel of his hard body beneath her fingertips, the whisper of her name on his lips, only those things were her reality now. She reached a hand out and stroked his jaw, feeling the slight roughness of his face, and the contact broke the floodgates.

She said nothing but, 'Jack.' It was enough. It was all they needed to make the months disappear completely, to give them the permission they needed to know each other again.

His voice was gravelly, dark with wanting her. 'Are you sure?'

She nodded, almost imperceptibly.

He stroked his hands over her arms and she shivered and clung to him, allowing him to raise her to her feet with one movement, clasping her hand in his as they moved silently to the bedroom.

Her head was reeling, not wanting to think or analyse, just wanting to fulfil the hunger that had been eating into her since they'd parted all those months ago. A hunger she'd tried to suppress, only to find it emerging now with renewed force, almost painful, like new scars breaking open, revealing the raw state of her heart beneath.

Jack sat on the edge of the bed, and she stood, trembling with anticipation, before him. He guided her towards him until she stood between his parted knees, pressing against the sides of her legs, holding her close. She shut her eyes for a moment, floating in the intimacy, then feeling his hand on her shirt, she opened her eyes and watched him as he took hold of the top button with his fingertips. He rubbed it gently, rolling it between thumb and forefinger, caressing it before easing it through the buttonhole and turning his attention to the next one.

Lauren gave a little sigh. The waiting was wonderful but it was torture at the same time because what she yearned for was for his fingertips to be caressing her. She made to undo the remaining buttons on her shirt but he gently lifted her hand away, and in the half-light she could see him shake his head, and he whispered, 'Patience is a virtue.'

He worked his way down until he pulled her shirt loose from her trousers and slipped the last button free. Her shirt opened to reveal the gentle curve of her stomach, the round globes of her breasts held in a simple white bra. Jack ran his hands across her stomach, holding her around the waist and dipping his head to press a kiss just below her navel, running his tongue down in a line from her navel to the top of her low-slung pants. Her eyes fluttered closed again, almost meditatively, focusing on the feel as his fingers worked the spell she knew so well, now easing the buttons on her trousers with the same slow caress. A doctor's hands, patient, skilled. The hands she'd been dreaming of, his touch the same that had woken her many nights in confused dreams that had felt real. And now it *was* real. Her breath caught in her throat as he reached the last button and traced a path in the opening that appeared, revealing the cotton of her underwear. She reached out for him, taking him by the hands and pulling him up towards her, willing him to stand up and take her in his arms.

He was standing so close now that their bodies were almost touching, yet not quite. The only physical connection were his hands now easing the clothes from her hips, bending to free her long limbs from the fabric until she stepped out of her clothes and stood before him, unabashed, naked, every nerve-ending tingling.

Now it was her turn, and she made herself take the same time he had, running her fingers over the fabric of his shirt, easing it from the waistband of his pants and slipping her fingers beneath to touch his skin. As she worked at his buttons, he bent to her and slipped an arm about her, encircling her in his warmth, lowering his mouth to cover hers in a kiss, slow and languorous. She all but melted, her hands stilling against his body as she lost herself in the wonder of him.

It had been so long since she'd felt like this, felt as though there was nothing and no one but them, wrapped in each other's arms. But there was plenty of time yet. She placed her hands on his broad chest to stop him. Smiling and pulling away, just a little, enough to slip his pants from his body, pull his shirt from his torso, revealing the body she knew so well, the body that had warmed her bed in her dreams for so many nights. A shiver ran through her, excitement for the moment, the here and now mixed with the bittersweet thought of all the moments they'd lost by being apart.

Their eyes met, and she held his gaze, mesmerised, allowed him to lay her on the bed, bending to kiss her fingers, stroke her body in long, reverent movements from her breast to her belly. He moved away and she watched as he bent down to the floor at the end of the bed. She heard a reassuring rustle and smiled, thinking, of course he'd be prepared, he was a careful man.

He lay on the bed next to her and caught her smile. He tucked a strand of dark hair behind her ear and whispered, 'Call me hopeful,' a smile playing around his lips.

Sliding an arm beneath her, he raised her head to meet his mouth, laying his other arm over her to cup her round breast in his hand. She felt his lips cover hers, caught the scent of him, warm and woodsy, and arched towards him as he circled her breast with slow, light strokes, in contrast to the increasing urgency of their kisses.

All the cares and troubles of the outside world ebbed away until she was riding with him on a wave of pleasure, skin against skin, lips on lips, the scents of their bodies mingling with the sheen on their skin. She explored his body as he explored hers, becoming familiar again with every inch. Her fear of being hurt again and her desire to keep him at a distance were washed away and she knew she was revealing everything in her heart, making herself vulnerable. But to have this moment it was worth risking all that and more. Those fears became small when held up to being with him again.

Several times Lauren felt herself swept up on a tremendous climactic wave but each time somehow they avoided the peak of their lovemaking, by tacit agreement wanting to extend the moment. How long was it that they teased each other with the offer of mutual ecstasy? Finally, they could wait no longer. He entered her with a gentleness that made her believe he'd always be with her and, as they started to move together, the room swam before her eyes. In unison they clung to one another and cried out, coming together with a dizzying force.

Did she melt into him, did they become one body and mind for a second in time? It felt as though they did and the magic of it lingered even as their breathing slowed and their muscles relaxed, their bodies easing into a closeness of a different kind. Lauren stretched out and turned on her side, wrapping one leg around Jack's calf. He slid an arm under her shoulders and pulled her into the crook of his arm, cradling her head against his bare chest and kissing her gently on her forehead. They fitted together perfectly. His breathing was already slowing. He was falling asleep, and going to sleep in each other's arms was undeniably the right thing to do. She'd go to sleep with a smile on her face tonight. There would be time enough in the morning to think about the wisdom of tonight's actions. For the next few hours at least, she'd pretend that all was right with the world.

Somewhere in the foggy recesses of her mind, Lauren could hear a bell ringing. Turning over to shut out the noise, her face hit a hard wall of muscle and her eyes snapped open as she remembered where she was. And with whom. Which would make that ringing noise her mobile phone, probably with two anxious new parents on the other end. She jumped out of bed and went into the main room where the light was still on, forgotten in their haste last night, and found her phone on the coffee table.

'Lauren speaking.'

'It's Tony. Sorry to bother you but Julie is a little concerned that Cooper's hungry. He won't stop crying.'

'That's nothing unusual, but I'll be right over.'

She tiptoed back into the bedroom and gathered up her clothes, just managing to see where everything was thanks to the light from the main room. A pale line of light was on the bed, too, and she watched the gentle rise and fall of Jack's chest. What a pity she had to go. There was nothing she'd like more than to curl up against him like a cat, warm and sated.

She stroked a hand over his bare chest and he stirred in his sleep, rolling over to reveal his broad back. What would it be like to wake up next to him every morning for the rest of her life? For the first time ever the years ahead seemed to stretch endlessly, now that she'd admitted just what Jack meant to her. Because, even if there was another time like last night, it would only be once or twice. Not for ever.

CHAPTER SIX

LAUREN dipped her cheek and snuggled a little closer. The bundle in her arms was, at half past six in the morning, finally silent and her fear of having it otherwise made her issue a low 'Shh,' as the outside door opened and first Steve then Jack appeared. They waved at her, nodding toward the baby in her arms, acknowledging the need for a warning to be quiet.

Steve headed straight for the kettle but Jack came to stand behind her, placing a hand on her shoulder as he looked down at baby Cooper nestled in her arms. His scent, clean and fresh, twisted its way around her and her heart did a few thousand flips when he bent down to drop a kiss on her hair. She'd never have thought Jack would do that, not with a colleague in the room. It made the action all the more meaningful.

He squatted beside her and said, his voice soft, 'We need to get Julie and Cooper checked up soon so we can get going. I'm on call-out again today.'

She nodded and felt a tumbling inside her as he sent her a crooked smile. Her tired mind received a direct energy hit. She could feel zinging going on all over her. Jack looked gorgeous. His hair was slightly damp and tousled. He'd obviously had time to wash but he hadn't shaved, and the faint shadow of a beard on his face added to his masculinity.

Lauren shifted the baby in her arms, checking that he was still sound asleep, before whispering back. 'I've just managed to settle Cooper so would you mind checking Julie first?'

He nodded again and touched her cheek lightly before he left the room.

'Silly,' Lauren muttered. Because it *was* ridiculous to feel bereft just because he'd left the room for a matter of moments.

'Here's your coffee. One for Jack, too.' Steve put two mugs on the kitchen table. As far as Lauren could tell, he was oblivious to the currents that had been zapping around the room. 'I'll go and check the plane so it's ready when you are.' He'd also obviously forgotten about Cooper, because he made no effort to lower his voice, but thankfully Cooper slept on.

Lauren leant back in her chair, enjoying the feel of a tiny baby cuddled in her arms, her mind drifting over the turn of events last night. A development she hadn't been expecting, as much as she now had to admit it was what she'd wanted, even knowing it wasn't the right thing to do. She couldn't get involved with him, she didn't want to risk having her heart broken again. But how strong was she meant to be? She shook her head.

One look from Jack and she went weak at the knees, one smile and she wanted to be in his arms, one touch and she melted. It had been an incredible night, exceeding even her memories—and there she'd been, trying to convince herself she'd imagined how amazing it had been. She suppressed a laugh as she tried to argue that it was the joy and mystery of the birth—arrivals of babies always tugged at her heart—which had been her undoing. But, no, there was no denying it. She had no willpower where Jack was concerned, not when push came to shove.

So, given the chance, she knew she'd do exactly the same thing again. Even though the feeling that life was exactly as it should be could only last for a short time, the memory could never be taken away from her. A tough act to follow, but if she was patient, surely one day she'd meet someone who made her feel like that but actually had the same dreams as her? Someone wonderful, just like Jack, but who was a country boy.

She let her eyes close and drifted off into a daydream of being held in the arms of her country man, the feel of him almost real. Her eyes flew open as she felt a touch on her arm and woke to look straight at that imaginary country man. But he was not so imaginary as it turned out, because even in her mind's eye he looked suspiciously like the man now standing in front of her.

'Sleepyhead.' Jack's voice was soft, caressing.

'Too much to think about to sleep.'

He smiled, his dimple appeared and the corners of his eyes crinkled. 'So I gathered. I thought when I woke to find you gone that I must have dreamed it.'

'Then it was one of the nicest dreams I've ever had.'

'Are you free tonight?'

'Yes.'

'Good. Then let's check Cooper. The sooner we start today, the sooner tonight comes.' He reached out to slip his arms around Cooper, lifting him from her, and he stood back to let her lead the way to Julie's room.

Lauren greeted the new parents then watched as Jack checked the baby, keeping up a steady stream of reassurances for Tony's and Julie's sake as he assessed their newborn. He moved with precision and he was infinitely gentle. He had a gift, she thought as she watched him palpate Cooper's head, checking his fontanelle and then placing a stethoscope over the little boy's chest to listen to his heart and lungs. The baby stirred in response to the cold metal, opening his eyes, and Lauren knew Jack was checking the baby's pupils for reaction to light. Next, he put on a disposable glove and slipped his little finger inside Cooper's mouth, checking his sucking and biting reflexes. Removing his glove, he checked the grasp reflex and then undid Cooper's nappy to check the umbilical cord, the testes, and perform the test for congenital hip dislocation. Cooper objected heartily to having his nappy removed.

'His hips seem fine.' Jack raised his voice over Cooper's cries. 'Is there any family history of hip trouble?'

Julie shook her head. 'Not on either side.'

Jack refastened Cooper's nappy before picking him up. Holding him under the arms, he pressed Cooper's feet down onto Julie's bedside table. Cooper lifted his legs up and down in a stepping motion.

'Look, he's walking!'

Lauren smiled at Tony's display of parental pride.

'I wish I could tell you how advanced he is but it's just a reflex in babies. It will be gone in a few weeks.' Jack laughed as he turned Cooper over. 'I've just got to check a couple more reflexes,' he said as he ran one finger lightly down Cooper's side from his ribs to his pelvis. Cooper obligingly curled towards Jack's touch.

'Great. Now, he won't like this next one much but I need to check that all his limbs are working equally.' He turned Cooper over so he was lying face up on Jack's left forearm with Jack's right hand supporting his head. Jack took his right hand away, lowering it an inch or two to catch Cooper's head again. Cooper wailed and flung his arms out wide, stretching his fingers and straightening his legs at the same time. 'A perfect response.'

Jack swaddled the baby quickly, his hands huge and dark against the white baby blanket. Lauren had a brief image of his hands on her skin and blinked hard to remove it. They had work to do.

'Everything looks fine,' Jack was saying to Julie as he returned her son to her for comforting. 'What are you going to do about postnatal visits? Coming into town for a stay?'

'My mum will be here by tomorrow and, unless we run into problems, we're planning to drive to Balcanoon for check-ups.'

'Who will you see there?' Jack hadn't heard of the town before but somehow it didn't sound large enough to offer postnatal support.

Lauren saw the looks of puzzlement on Tony's and Julie's faces and explained to Jack. 'We do a regular clinic there, usually the second Wednesday in the month. Julie just needs to make an appointment.' To the parents, she said, 'And remember you can always speak to us over the radio if you're worried about anything.'

As they were finishing, Steve knocked and put his head around the door to let them know the plane was ready.

Farewells said, they left the new family behind, the image of the three of them snuggled down together in bed adding to Lauren's sense of contentment. Striding along, with Steve on one side and Jack on the other, she was also aware how good it felt to have Jack beside her. She was looking forward to talking about last night. What was going through his head? Had it changed anything between them?

Steve touched her on the arm. 'Did you hear me?'

She laughed. 'No. I think I'm asleep on my feet.' She avoided looking at Jack as she made the excuse for her distraction. 'What did you say?'

'Have we got time for a shower back at base before we head out again?'

'I don't fancy a full day of clinics without one. It won't matter if we're a little behind schedule.'

'Are we staying back late tonight?'

Lauren could feel Jack's interest pique. Oops. She hadn't quite got around to telling him the full story about her teenage mothers' support groups. And she was pretty sure he wasn't going to like it.

Maybe she could wriggle out of it by leaving it vague. She made a noncommittal 'Mmm' sound.

'Why would you already know you're going to have to stay late?'

Then again, maybe she wasn't going to wriggle out of it.

Steve looked over the top of Lauren's head in Jack's direction. 'You haven't done a clinic run with Lauren before?'

Jack shook his head. Lauren turned to Steve so Jack couldn't see her and widened her eyes at him, hoping the message would get through. They were almost at the plane. If she could stall for a moment or two, maybe Jack would have forgotten his question by the time they'd boarded.

Unfortunately, all Steve did was send a puzzled look her way before continuing. 'She came up with this idea of staying late after remote clinics to run her support groups, so the kids in outlying areas could come.' They had reached the plane and Steve started to get things ready for boarding.

Jack remained silent. Somehow she doubted that was a good sign.

She thought about sitting with Steve but if Jack had an issue, that sort of tactic wouldn't put him off. He was as stubborn as her. The moment they were in the air, Jack turned to her. 'Mind filling me in on what Steve was talking about?'

'You're not going to make a big deal of it, are you? I thought you'd agreed there was a need for the groups and that they were well run.'

'We were talking about your spare time then and you know it.'

'This is my spare time, too. It's after-hours when the remote clinics finish. All it means is staying back for an hour or so before flying back to town. The others involved, the pilots and any other medicos who attended the clinic, all agree to it, they support it.'

He sighed—and she found herself trying to interpret the sound. Was he exasperated? Frustrated with her? Angry?

'Number one, I have no doubt you didn't give them any other option but to go along with it.'

From his voice, she was guessing he was exasperated, frustrated *and* angry.

The set of his jaw seemed to back that up, too. 'And number two, whether you all agree or not is irrelevant. You're there in an AAS plane, with AAS staff. What you're doing amounts to an abuse of AAS resources.' There was an edge of steel in his words that Lauren hadn't heard before, but she wasn't backing down. This was too close to her heart.

'You're being ridiculous.'

'I haven't finished.' He cut her off. 'What happens if there's an emergency call-out and you've effectively commandeered the plane and staff for your own purposes? What happens if there's an accident with one of the AAS staff or something goes wrong during the clinic? Whose insurance covers that? You have no authority to be there or to run the group.'

Heat swept through her, not least because she had to admit she'd never given any thought to something as boring as insurance. Feeling backed into a corner, her instinct was fight, not flight.

'The plane used on the clinic run is hardly ever needed for emergencies, that's what the on-call roster is for. But *if* we were needed, then, of course, the session would be cancelled. You're just jumping all over it because it's a little outside the square and you can't categorise it.' Who cared if she was hitting below the belt, making it personal? 'What do you know about life in the country? You've already agreed these girls badly need support of this kind, but then you deny it just because they're geographically isolated. That's the whole point of the AAS in the first place, ensuring access to health care despite enormous distances and isolation.'

'*Medical* care. It's outside the AAS charter to run around the country taking on social causes.'

For a second she was dumbstruck with fury. Mentally she rolled up her sleeves and prepared for round two. 'Call it playing at social causes if you want, it just highlights your ignorance of the issues. We're *there* on the spot, in regional areas these young women can actually reach. They can't get into town, that's the point. Are you saying we should just thumb our noses at them and fly off?' She was trying hard to keep her voice level but she could feel her anger getting the better of her again and she talked on, ignoring his attempt to get a word in. 'We can make a difference! But apparently that doesn't mean anything to suits from the city—you just want to be able to make lists and tick stupid little boxes.' She unbuckled her seat belt and stood up. 'You can tick your boxes all you want, you've got no say over me and what I do.'

Stalking up to the cockpit, she saw Steve flick a glance

at her. Thankfully, true to his nature, he said nothing about the thundercloud she knew was on her face.

Jack watched Lauren slip into the seat next to Steve before lying back in his seat, eyes closed, trying to shut out the image of Lauren's angry face. Who would have believed that just a few hours ago they'd been lying in each other's arms? He did agree that her social groups were a good idea but that was when she had been using her spare time. Commandeering AAS staff and equipment for her own personal use was an entirely different matter. She was nothing if not stubborn, but surely even she'd see that when she'd had time to calm down?

He liked to play by the rules, at least as far as work was concerned. She was an employee of a large organisation, he was amazed she'd been able to run these clinics without approval for as long as she had. She just assumed she'd get her own way but she'd have to learn to play by the rules, too. Perhaps once he got her to the city she'd get involved with other projects that were more clear cut.

Lauren was a challenge to him, a challenge to his way of thinking, his way of working and his way of relaxing. He had needed a new challenge but had been planning on having a professional, not personal one. But he wasn't about to give up. He was realising more and more every day that for once letting his heart rule his head in making his snap decision to come to Port Cadney had been the wisest move he'd ever made. Seeing her again had been the only proof he'd needed. Last night had set it in stone. And if he was learning that the battle was going to be harder to win than he'd ever contemplated, he was also learning he wanted her more than he'd ever wanted anything before.

And what was worth having was worth sticking your

neck out for. He settled down in his seat, his resolve firm. Whatever it took, Lauren was going to be by his side when he left this place.

Lauren was exhausted when she and Steve arrived back in town at the end of a long day of clinics. Normally she had plenty of energy even after the extra teenage mothers' group but it had been a busy day on top of a busy night. She was looking forward to a quiet evening and she felt less out of sorts than this morning—Jack would have had some time to reflect on how wrong he'd been. He'd asked if she was free tonight so perhaps she'd be able to see him and clear the air, settle their earlier disagreement in her favour, accept his apology with good grace. After all, he was still new out here, she had to make allowances for that. As she filed away the paperwork, Sheila approached.

'This fax just came for you.' She handed Lauren a piece of paper. Glancing at the AAS letterhead, she saw it was a fax from Central Headquarters in Adelaide.

She read through it and could feel the rigidity return to her body. 'You've got to be kidding,' she muttered as she finished rereading it and the message really sank in.

'What is it?'

'Martin—' she named the Medical Director for Central Operations '—wants me to submit a proposal about putting my remote teenage mothers' groups onto the AAS clinic schedule.'

'But that's good, isn't it? It would mean you'd get some funding.'

'But he's also said that I'm not to run any more meetings until a decision has been made.' She stared sightlessly at the paper in her hands. 'Where's Jack? I bet he's behind this. I've got a few things to say to him.' She

knew she'd piqued Sheila's curiosity with her outburst—
the woman's open mouth was a dead give-away—but she
really didn't care.

'He's gone to Adelaide with a transfer.'

'Damn.'

'If he's got any sense he'll stay there.' Sheila's sense
of humour bounced back. 'He'd be safer.'

Lauren arrived at her parents' house midmorning, hug-
ging her mum, glad she had a rostered day off. She was
in desperate need of fresh air and open spaces today.

'Good morning, love. You look tired.'

Lauren kissed her mother before answering. 'I'm OK,
just looking forward to taking Molly out for a ride.'

Her mum gave her an extra squeeze but didn't push
the issue. 'Perhaps you could take your father his morning tea, I've just about finished packing it.'

'Sure. Where is he?'

'Gone to fix the windmill in the side paddock, the one
next to Fitzpatrick's.' Margaret kept talking to her youngest daughter as she continued wrapping sandwiches and
cake. 'I've told him to leave it for Mick, but you know
your father, doesn't think anyone can do as good a job
as him.'

'Why did he employ Mick if he won't hand over some
of the work?'

'Good question. Why don't you ask him? He's a stubborn one, your father, must be where you get it from.'
She handed Lauren a large, insulated lunch bag and a
flask. 'Off you go, there's enough tea in there for two.
I'll see you for lunch.'

A little later Lauren reined Molly in and dismounted
in the shadow of the windmill, calling out to her father.

'I've brought your tea, Dad.'

'Great, I'll just tighten this bolt and I'll be right down.'

Lauren shielded her eyes from the sun as she watched her father climb down the steel framework of the windmill. The last cross-brace was three feet from the ground and Frank jumped the distance. As he landed, Lauren saw his right leg give way and heard him yell out as he landed heavily on his side. Almost immediately he tried to sit up.

'Don't move.' She ran to his side. 'What happened?'

'My leg, it just gave way.'

Lauren squatted down next to him. His right leg was lying at an awkward angle and it looked a good inch or two shorter than his left leg.

'I suspect you've fractured your hip.' He was half-lying, half-sitting, his hands clasped around his right thigh, and she could see from his pale complexion and the beads of sweat on his face that he was in pain.

'Keep still. Let me check you out.'

She felt his pulse and counted his respirations, relieved that both were within normal range. Next she checked his femoral and ankle pulses and again was conscious of her relief to feel them present, indicating that blood supply to the leg hadn't been compromised. Her skipping heart slowed down a touch with the realisation.

'I can't find anything too disastrous. Are you hurting anywhere else?' Frank shook his head. 'Don't move your leg, I'm just going to get something to keep you warm.'

Running to her dad's ute, she grabbed an oilskin coat from the back.

She returned to his side. 'It's not as good as a blanket but it'll trap some body heat. I know you're not comfortable, but stay still while I radio the AAS and Mum.'

She couldn't recall ever seeing her dad vulnerable before and it was hard to stay cool and calm. It was definitely not like treating the average patient, not when personal emotions were involved.

Three heads turned as Peter Wilson walked into the cubicle, x-rays in hand. 'OK, Frank, you've managed to fracture the neck of your femur, as Lauren suspected, but there's no other damage that we can find. Unfortunately you'll need surgery but the orthopaedic surgeon isn't back in town for five days and this type of surgery can't wait. The good news is there's an AAS plane available now to fly you down to Adelaide for surgery today.'

'You call that good news? How long is all this going to take?'

Lauren suppressed a smile. The painkillers were clearly working given that her dad was back calling a spade a spade.

The doctor slid the X-ray onto the light-box, pointing at a spot just below a ball-shaped bone. 'See this line running down here? That's your fracture. It's quite unstable in weight-bearing which is why you couldn't walk on it. The hip joint is a ball and socket joint. This round part is the top of your leg, the ball component. That fits into the socket which is, fortunately, still intact. Surgery involves replacing the head and neck of the femur with a metal prosthesis. You'll be in hospital for up to a week, depending on your recovery rate, but you can be transferred back to Port Cadney if you're not ready to go home.'

'What about the farm?'

'You shouldn't expect to be out and about on the farm for about six weeks. Heavy work will be out altogether.'

'Don't worry about all that now.' Margaret held Frank's hand. 'Mick can manage, that's what he's there for.'

Peter continued, 'It's a bit difficult to give you a time-line for recovery right now, there are lots of variables. There's often damage to the blood supply to the hip, which can cause complications if it's not addressed quickly, so you do need to go to Adelaide for surgery. I'd advise you to consent to the surgery and we'll arrange transport to Adelaide.'

'OK, OK, show me where to sign.'

Peter handed over the paperwork, indicating where he needed Frank's signature.

Lauren took her mother aside. 'Why don't we go home and you can speak to Mick and pack a bag of things for you and Dad? We can catch a flight down this afternoon.'

'Could you fly down with your father?'

'Depending on the flight schedule and how full the plane is, I could.'

Her mother nodded. 'I'd be happier if one of us could go with him, make sure he's OK. It might take me a while to get things sorted at home. I'll get down there as quickly as I can.'

'OK.' She squeezed her mum tight. 'I'll see what I can do.'

There was still half an hour until her mother's flight was due to arrive so Lauren ducked into the AAS hangar at the Adelaide Airport to kill some time and have a chat with whoever was about. Now that her father had been taken into Theatre, she needed some distraction. And a break. It hadn't been the most enjoyable few hours she'd ever spent and the adrenalin surge had left her feeling washed out.

As she headed for the administration office within the hangar, the adrenalin she'd thought she was all out of came back with force as Jack stepped out of the office.

'You!' Her hands clenched at her sides and she felt the rush of blood to her face. 'What are you playing at, telling Martin about my teenage mothers' sessions?'

'What are you talking about?'

She watched as the big grin that had lit up his face when he'd spotted her disappeared. 'Martin wants a submission and I assume you were the one who told him.' Somewhere in her mind she knew this wasn't the time or the place, but that didn't seem as important as fighting for her cause. 'What I do in my own time is my business.'

'Not when you're using AAS resources.'

'Everyone's there voluntarily, it's not costing the AAS one cent.'

'That's partly my point. If you're going to run these clinics, you may as well be getting remunerated for it. I'm sure everyone else you've involved would appreciate it.'

He appeared to be remaining calm and unflustered. It only irritated her more.

'So you did tell him.'

'Yes, but not to make trouble. You know I agree there's a need for the sessions but I also think there's an appropriate way to go about things.'

She gritted her teeth, willing the stress that she knew was ringing in every word she spoke to settle down. But this was just not what she needed on top of her dad's accident. 'Even if it means that I can't run my groups until a decision has been made.'

'I don't know anything about that.'

'No, of course not. You just set the whole ''appropriate procedures'' treadmill going without considering the consequences. Are you going to explain to the mums why the sessions have been cancelled?'

'I'd be happy to. I'd like to come with you to see one

of the remote sessions anyway, but I'm not prepared to do it in a clandestine manner.'

'Everything by the book?'

'If I'm going to be the new medical director for Central Operations, then I need to make sure I dot the Is and cross the Ts.'

'The new medical director?' Surely she hadn't heard right?

Apparently she had.

'Martin's retiring and I've applied for the job. It's the next step for me.'

'Sounds like you think you've got it in the bag.'

'I think I have a better than average chance.'

'So, ultimately, the fate of my clinics will rest with you?'

'If I get the position, yes.'

'That makes it worse. You told me you were on my side!'

'I am on your side but protocol has to be followed. I can't give you special dispensation just because...' He paused, searching for the words. 'Just because we've slept together. That's not the way I operate, and I wouldn't think you'd want any special favours either.'

The fact that Jack wouldn't bend the rules for her didn't upset her as much as his casual description of their relationship. 'I see. So a few months in town, just enough time to upset the apple cart and rekindle an old flame, before you head off to bigger and better things. Is that it?'

'Don't go putting words in my mouth again. I didn't come to Port Cadney to cause trouble.'

'No. It was a brief stop for you on your road to career success.'

'There's more to it than that.'

'I doubt it. Tell me, if you get this job, how much longer are you planning on staying in Port Cadney?'

'Would you miss me?'

'Would that matter?' She knew she'd been ignoring the fact that he'd go one day. She'd thought they'd have more time. Despite their differences of opinion, she'd let herself believe he had real feelings for her. Had her judgement been completely wrong? 'It seems I'm just a way to help you pass the time. Is that it?'

CHAPTER SEVEN

JACK took one look at Lauren's face and knew he had seconds to calm her down before her barely contained fury erupted. Where to start? He ran his fingers through his hair, leaving it standing every which way, like a mass of baby bird feathers.

'No, that's not it, not by a long shot, but now isn't the time to talk about us.' He glanced around them, reminding Lauren of their very public location.

'I don't care where we are. Just give me a straight answer.'

He should've known their whereabouts wouldn't hold much sway over her. He held his hands out, palms facing up, signalling his desire to put this conversation off to another time, another place. 'I doubt anything I say right now will matter. You've got it all worked out without me saying a word. I'm unlikely to make things better if I start talking.' He wasn't looking for a fight. That was the last thing he wanted, but from the set of her shoulders, the tension in her body, the words she was using, it all spelt trouble.

'So that's it? No discussion? No explanation? No *apology*?'

'We'll talk in town.'

'Don't think this is the end of it.'

'I'd be shocked if it was.' He was managing to keep his cool in the face of her anger. After all, it was understandable that she was upset. It just hadn't occurred to him that she'd be quite this annoyed.

'You're insufferable.' She turned on her heel and stalked off.

He almost laughed out loud at her insistence on having the last word. It was so…Lauren. And Lauren was so…utterly gorgeous. Quite how that could be when she was more furious than he'd even seen her before, he couldn't say. But she was. He watched as she walked out of the hangar. And only after she turned a corner and vanished from view did he realise that he didn't even know what she was doing in Adelaide.

The following evening, Jack stared out of the plane window, watching in a trance-like state as the colours of the setting sun played over the red sands below. They were still a good hour away from arriving back at base at the end of that day's work. Plenty of time for reflection. He'd felt awful when he'd heard about Lauren's father. The last thing she would have needed was an argument with him, on top of her other worries. Perhaps it was a good thing that they hadn't seen each other yet. Hopefully it would have given them both time to calm down. He smiled as one very angry face appeared before his mind's eye. Perhaps the more time she had for calming down, the better. Had he ever known another woman so firmly convinced what she was doing was right? He loved that about her, loved that she'd fight for what she believed in, that she was so fully alive and involved in what she was doing. There were no half-measures with Lauren. But she did need to learn to go about things in the right way.

But was he being a stick-in-the-mud, insisting that things be done by the book? He had to admit he hadn't thought about that possibility before presenting the issue to management. But he'd been right, he was sure of it.

And, even faced with Lauren's anger, he'd do the same thing again. He certainly wasn't about to go against his principles because of undue pressure from her. That was the way disaster lay.

He rubbed his temples, working through the myriad questions he was posing for himself. Anyone who could have him second-guessing his own decisions was trouble. Once he made a decision he never thought to question it. She was the most exhausting, desirable woman he'd ever met. She'd got under his skin, into his head and into his bed. He'd have to tread carefully to make sure he didn't end up making mistakes.

Ryan slapped Jack on the back as he sank the black ball, winning them the game of pool against a pair of locals in the pub. They shook hands with their opponents and headed for the bar.

'It's my shout. What's your joy?'

'Make it a light, thanks.'

Jack took the cold beer from Ryan and they clinked their bottles in a toast.

'I could get used to this.'

'Beer?'

Jack laughed and shook his head. 'No, the country ritual of a few beers and a game of something, tennis, pool, whatever, at the end of a day. The winding-down process.'

Jack grinned at Ryan's mystified expression.

'You don't do this in the city?'

'I'm sure some people do, I just never had the time.' Not really the case, he knew, but the truth—that he'd never *made* the time—seemed lame. He certainly never imagined that he would make time to shoot some pool with a girlfriend's ex! But he and Ryan got along well in spite of their history with Lauren.

Making time to wind down had never seemed important in the city. Why was it now? It didn't fit his self-image: career man on a fast track to success. The thought he'd had before of Lauren as a siren of the sea came back to him and hit him hard. Was she leading him away from his chosen path? If she was, it was proving almost impossible to resist.

Ryan appeared to still be digesting Jack's alternative attitude to work and play. 'I'm not sure there's any point in working if you don't get to enjoy switching off at the end of the day.'

'Other than the other minor benefit of earning a salary.' That was better. That was the answer of a driven career-man.

'Compared to the taste of a cold one at the end of the day, it just doesn't come close.' He looked over Jack's shoulder and waved. 'Over here.'

Jack swivelled on his bar stool and his chest tightened with anticipation, hoping there wouldn't be another fight. It was Chloe, with Lauren at her side.

'How's your dad?' Jack and Ryan spoke in unison but it didn't go unnoticed by Jack that her reply was directed solely at Ryan.

'The op went well. Mum's stayed down there.'

Chloe sent what seemed to be a sympathetic smile Jack's way. Great, so Lauren was clearly mad enough to have told her friend about their encounter in Adelaide.

'And the farm?' Ryan asked.

'I came back this morning and headed out there.' She chewed on her bottom lip. 'The farmhands say they can manage in the short term but...' The comment was left hanging in the air.

'What do you think your dad will do?'

She shrugged. 'Who knows? He'll probably be back trying to run things next week, he's so stubborn.'

Chloe nudged Jack's arm and nodded at Lauren. 'That's where she gets it from.'

Jack chose to ignore the comment. It seemed wise to stick to safer topics. 'What would you like to drink?'

'Actually, I'm starving. Who wants to get dinner?' Chloe patted her stomach and Jack noticed with interest how eager Ryan was to take her up on her suggestion.

He stood up and walked over to Chloe, dropping his arm loosely around her shoulders. 'You guys don't want to come?'

They were off out of the pub before Lauren could protest about being left alone with Jack. Which he guessed she'd been about to do because she was looking even more put out.

'They seem very chummy all of a sudden.'

Lauren didn't answer. She sat down on Ryan's stool and ordered a beer.

'You'll have to talk to me at some stage.'

She turned to him, one eyebrow raised, 'As I recall, I was trying to do that yesterday.'

He laughed and watched as the colour rose in her cheeks. 'As *I* recall, you weren't trying to do anything of the sort. You were trying to browbeat me into submission.'

He watched as she bit down on her lip, trying to squelch the tiny smile that was threatening to appear.

'I'm sorry about your dad. How is he really?'

'One minute in denial, the next furious.' She shook her head, and he watched, fascinated, as her dark hair swung about her shoulders, bare but for the tiny straps of her fitted cotton top.

'A bit like you?'

'There's no denial, Jack. I'm going to get these clinics.' Her voice was soft but the light shining in her eyes was anything but.

'And I was trying to help you. I don't want to fight about this. I can think of more pleasant ways to get what you want.'

'You're not trying to sweet-talk me, are you?'

He laughed, perfect white teeth flashing in contrast to his brown skin. 'I hope I'm never so stupid as to think I can sweet-talk you into anything. What I'm saying is, I agree there's a need for your groups but I think they should be added to the official clinic runs rather than just being tagged on the end, which has meant everyone is effectively doing unpaid overtime.' He leaned in closer, fixing his eyes on hers, trying to ensure his message got through to her. 'Secondly, I wasn't just being a thorn in your side when I raised the issue of insurance. What would have happened in the event of an accident? You have no authority to be there at that time and you can't just assume injuries would be covered by AAS insurance.'

Lauren took a deep breath. It went against all her instincts to say what she was about to say. 'I concede you're right on that point.'

'Pardon?'

She glared at him and he laughed again, raising his hands in mock surrender.

'OK, I heard you. It was just such a rare admission that I wanted to hear it again.'

'Don't hold your breath.'

She couldn't believe she was even having this conversation with the very man who had tried to sabotage her project. She glanced at him, his head tilted back as he drank from his almost empty bottle. His skin was noticeably darker than it had been on his arrival in town and he looked even more handsome, if that was possible. He looked…relaxed? Was that the difference? He lowered his head and put his bottle on the bar and she still couldn't take her eyes off him. It made no sense at all. Why was she even sitting here? It made no sense at all. None of it.

It seemed he could read her mind.

'I can't say I thought we'd be having a semi-convivial drink tonight. But I'm very glad we are.' His smile shot straight through her, sending shock waves from her head to her toes.

'You said you were trying to help me get my clinics back on the drawing board. What did you mean? But don't think I'm letting you off the hook for going behind my back with this.' She added to her mental list his other misdemeanours, which were rapidly piling up. Applying for jobs and not telling her, planning to leave town and not letting her know. They were all pretty major things. And they added up to the fact that he didn't see her as anything more than a short-term fling. What else hadn't he told her?

'I don't think I did,' Jack said, 'but we'll leave that for another day, OK?' She didn't answer. 'Have you started your proposal for management to consider?'

'Of course.'

'Have you done one before?'

For the first time she could feel her mask of confidence slipping. 'No.'

'How would you feel about me looking at it before you send it off? I have a good idea what they'll be looking for.'

She bit down on the smart retort that sprang to her

lips. This wasn't the time for more fights. She needed every bit of help she could get to guarantee the success of her funding. 'Thanks. How about now?'

'You've done enough of it already?'

'I've finished going over my first draft.'

She could see from his eyes that he was impressed with her tenacity. And when he told her so, she could feel the ice start to thaw a fraction.

'I've got it here.' She kicked the daypack propped up against her feet. 'It's cooling down outside and there'll be a table in the courtyard.'

'Let's go.'

'You've covered aims and objectives, proposed structure for the groups. You've argued your need for extra support from a psychologist or social worker and occasional medical support, and your anticipated outcomes are strong, very persuasive.' Jack tapped the pile of papers on the table between them. 'But what about your costing? Do you think it's as solid as it can be?'

'What do you suggest?'

'You want Martin to read this and know that you've thought about where every cent is going and that you haven't forgotten anything. He doesn't want to be hit with unexpected claims when he's done his budget. Or have any doubts as to what the money will be spent on.'

It occurred to her that if he took the job it would be Jack who had to deal with that. But he'd probably already thought about that. On top of which they didn't need another issue to argue about now. Nothing was more important than her groups.

'Budgeting isn't my strong point. Any pointers?'

He bent his head over the paper and started to scribble figures and equations, occasionally throwing a question her way. Finally, he straightened up in his chair and turned the paper to her, pushing it across the table. She leant across and took it, their fingers touching briefly. Maybe it was a good thing he would be going soon. Even watching him doing maths had been riveting.

She read through the figures, trying to forget about the fact that his hand was still resting on the table and if she wanted, she could slip her fingers under his.

'It's good. Thank you. Will it do, the proposal as a whole, I mean?'

He nodded. 'I think it's all there. But it still comes down to whether there's any money in the budget this year—you might have to wait. And, of course, there are management's own personal convictions. They might not think this cause is worth their attention.'

'Like you.'

'If you recall, I came around pretty quickly once you sold it to me, and I'm pretty hard to convince. Plus, your anticipated objectives section is great, like I said. I'd be surprised if Martin doesn't give you the green light.'

'I hope you're right. And there're a lot of young women out there who hope so, too.'

'Speaking of which, Martin has agreed to let you do one more clinic so you can at least tell some of the girls face to face what is happening.'

'Fantastic. There's a group tomorrow I was going to have to cancel.'

A sigh of relief ran through him as he watched the animation return to her face, her good humour apparently semi-restored. 'We're on clinic together tomorrow so I'll be able to see you in action.'

She gathered up her papers. 'Thanks for your help just now. I'm going to go type it up and fax it off to head-quarters tonight. When do you think I might hear?'

He shrugged. 'I don't know. But you can always follow it up with e-mails every couple of weeks or so.'

'You think it might take weeks?'

'These things usually do.'

Automatically, he pushed his chair back and stood the moment she made a move to stand. She stood there opposite him, tapping her foot, and when she bit her bottom lip, he couldn't take his eyes off her. Man, but he wanted to be the one nibbling on her lips. Given what he'd just done to her support groups, it didn't seem likely to happen any time soon. And they hadn't even touched on him leaving town for the city. All in all, it was a miracle she'd even talked to him tonight.

When she reached up and gave him a quick hug, he was so taken aback he didn't have time to react. It seemed to take her by surprise, too, because she grabbed her daypack and almost ran out of the courtyard.

Lauren clapped her hands and the five young women present stopped talking and gave her their full attention. They were all sitting in a circle on chairs in Pimba's small community hall, having gathered there at the end of the day's remote clinic. Jack had already met two of the women when he'd given them their antenatal checkups. He'd had to come down heavy on one of them, Bev, who wasn't taking care of herself, or her unborn baby. And from the sulky way she was glowering at him she wasn't going to forgive him in a hurry.

'Its great to see you all today. Four of you I know, and we have one new face.' Lauren was smiling at one young girl who Jack was certain couldn't be any older than fifteen. On paper, he agreed this sample of the population needed their attention, but when faced with some of the girls in real life he couldn't help but be shocked at how young they were to be facing one of life's biggest challenges. He certainly wouldn't have coped at their age with something so huge.

He looked around at the faces as Lauren continued, setting the tone for the session with her warm voice, bringing the newcomer into the fold with a gentle and caring touch. 'Welcome. I'm Lauren, I'm a flight nurse and this is Jack, he's a flying doctor. What's your name?'

'Katie.' It was a whisper and she looked on the verge of tears, but it was a start.

'We're glad you're here, Katie.'

The others chorused their agreement and Jack felt out of his depth, one lone representative of the gender who was half responsible for this but nowhere to be seen. He knew these groups were for women only, but for the first time he wondered where the fathers-to-be were and what role they would play in their children's lives. Any? How did you work out the expected involvement of a father who was probably little more than a child himself?

He blinked hard to bring himself back to the group. The last thing they needed was to see someone in authority who wasn't paying any attention to them at all.

Lucky he'd started to listen again, because Lauren was talking about him. 'He's just here to learn about what we do, the sort of thing you guys need from us, so he can go to our bosses and make sure we get it.' She turned to him and her smile was dazzling, daring him to go against what she'd just said.

All he could do was grin and say hello to the group. He had to hand it to her. Clearly she had no intention of telling them about the question mark hanging over her project. Sure, he could be the bad guy and make that announcement, but he'd bet his precious book collection she'd been sure he wouldn't. Which meant she probably had plans to have him all stitched up by the time they got back to town. He hated to think of the pressure that she was likely to bring to bear on him to get her way. Thank heavens he'd omitted to tell her he was here on behalf of management. Martin wanted a first-hand report and Jack's opinion on what he saw today would count for a lot in the final decision. Despite that, he stayed silent. He needed to pay attention. But what if he didn't like what he saw?

'It's going to be less structured this time than when I last saw you.' To Katie, she added, 'Last time, we had Nadine with us. She's a psychologist so when she's able to be here, we can work on strategies to help you deal with your thoughts and feelings and also how to cope with the reactions of others. But we can still link you up with her to have chats over the phone if you ever want some extra help in between these groups.'

She stopped and smiled at them and it seemed to Jack that even Katie's apparent terror edged down a notch in the face of Lauren's genuine warmth.

'Becky, you had some ideas for today's session. Do you want to kick it off?'

'Your notes on who to see about money and stuff was good, and I've talked to the welfare agency on the phone. But I'm having a really tough time with my olds—' Jack assumed she meant her parents '—and I don't know if I can keep on living there.'

A girl who had been introduced as Jodi, who had been the only one to smile at Jack so far, asked, 'Did they kick you out?'

Becky shook her head. 'But I reckon it won't be far away. My stepdad says he's already got a nagging wife and me to put up with, and he's not having a screaming brat as well.'

The conversation went on and on, and with each new insight into the strain and stresses they faced on a daily basis Jack felt more and more like an absolute heel for not immediately supporting Lauren in her quest to help this group of young women.

He watched with admiration as Lauren guided them, questioned them, helped them to generate alternative approaches and ways around their problems. It was a tough group. It was clear she'd put a lot of effort into winning their trust and that the participation he was seeing was the result of hours of effort on her part. It was also clear she'd built up a skill base outside her nursing training. Her counselling skills were impressive. Even Katie was looking marginally less terrified. Had Lauren learnt it all from experience or had she taken additional study on as well? It was another example of her tenacious approach to life. She never did anything by halves. When was the last time he'd shown such commitment to something outside his own career goals? Had he ever?

'It's almost time to call it a day. But before we do—' she caught Jack's eye '—I thought you might like to hear what it's like for a new mum. Is that still all right with you, Jodi?'

Jack smelt a rat but there wasn't much he could do about it. She must have planned this with Jodi before the session.

'Sure. Because you guys—' she nodded to three of her four peers '—haven't actually had your babies yet, I thought you might like to know what it's been like for me. Not about having no sleep and changing nappies and stuff, but what sort of reaction you're going to get from other people. You probably already have a fair idea of your families' reactions, good or bad.' She smiled around the group. 'But what about strangers in town, your neighbours, people on the other end of the phone when you've got to ring up and ask something about the baby?'

'You mean it doesn't get better when the baby comes? I'm still going to have the looks and the comments?' Tina groaned.

'I'm not trying to get you down. It will get better, because you'll love your baby so much, but it's still hard when other people judge you, put you down just 'cos you're young. Like the oldies are the only ones who know how to love.'

They all laughed, showing exactly what they thought of that idea.

'But you need to be prepared for having your feelings hurt and also to get tougher and stand up for yourself. Don't let anyone make you feel you can't be the best parent in the whole world just because you're young.'

'I'm worried they'll take my baby away.'

The whole group stopped and turned to look at the youngest member, the only one who had so far been almost silent.

'Who's going to do that, Katie?' Lauren had taken over, talking gently to coax Katie out of herself.

'Welfare. They took me away from Mum and my life's been bad ever since. I don't want that to happen to my baby. She'll be my only family.'

Jack felt a lump about the size of a football swell up in his throat. Had this young woman become pregnant just so she'd have someone to love?

'That would be a really scary thought to have hanging over your head,' said Lauren.

The tears slid down Katie's face and she looked resolutely down at her slim hands folded in her lap. Jodi slipped out of her chair and squatted next to her, wrapping an arm around her childishly narrow shoulders.

'Where are you living now, Katie?' Jack watched Lauren. He could see she was looking for something here but he wasn't sure what.

'Nowhere. I got kicked out of my aunt's this morning. I stay there between foster-homes but she won't have me full time. And now she's found out about the baby, she says she won't have me at all.'

Lauren nodded at the other girls who seemed to understand the session was over and rose without saying a word, although they all patted Katie on the shoulder as they walked out of the room. Jack took a little longer to get the hint that he wasn't needed right now. It wasn't until Jodi caught his eye and jerked her head towards the door that he realised he should go, too.

Which left Lauren with Katie. And given that he had absolutely no idea what options a kid like Katie had in these circumstances, it was the best thing all around.

It was another hour before Lauren arrived back at the airstrip.

'Sorry to keep you waiting.'

Steve answered, 'No problem. Ready to go?'

She nodded and they boarded, Lauren motioning for Jack to sit up front with Steve. Was she eager to avoid a conversation she must know they had to have?

When they arrived back at base, it was Jack's turn to avoid her. There was a phone call he had to make and he slipped away to the office.

'A few of us are going to play tennis—would you like to come?' Lauren had followed him.

He replaced the receiver halfway through dialling the number and turned to face her, suspecting she was only there so she could start phase two of her campaign to persuade him to go to bat on behalf of her groups.

'I've got a few calls to make first. How about I meet you there?'

She narrowed her eyes slightly. Was she weighing up whether he, too, was playing a few games? They still hadn't had their conversation about him leaving to take up the Adelaide post. Hopefully she'd attribute the phone calls to that. Eventually she nodded and left.

He made his call and afterwards he stood for some time, staring unseeingly down at the desk. There were so many unfinished conversations hanging in the air between them that he could itemise them only with difficulty. Issue one: he was leaving town. Two: he'd been stupid enough not to tell her, thinking it was better to wait until he knew what was happening. Three: he'd assumed she'd come, too, but would she? Four: the future of her teenage mothers' groups.

His head was spinning. He wasn't even sure that there weren't more issues they needed to resolve. And he certainly wasn't sure of the answers. But what could he do other than take it one step at a time?

'Yes!' Lauren punched the air with her fist as Jack's return won them the match.

'Is that tennis etiquette?'

She laughed in reply and they walked side by side to the net to shake hands.

Jack extended his hand to shake first Chloe's then Ryan's outstretched hands. 'Sorry about my partner being a poor winner.'

'We're used to it, mate,' said Ryan.

Lauren poked Ryan with her racket over the net. 'Coming in for a drink?'

Ryan and Chloe shook their heads. 'We've got something else on.'

Jack flicked a glance at Lauren as the others walked off.

'What do you think of that development?' Jack asked, inclining his head in Ryan's direction.

'I hope it works out for them. Ryan deserves to be happy.'

'It doesn't bother you at all?'

'Why should it? Chloe's a much better match for him than I ever was. Ryan's like a brother to me, we never should have dated.'

'Then why did you?'

'Everyone seemed to expect us to. It just sort of happened.'

Jack searched her face. There was nothing there to suggest she had a problem with Ryan dating Chloe. Hopefully that meant that chapter in her life was closed. At least her gait was light next to his as they walked into the club. There weren't any outward signs he could read that suggested she was affected at all by the blossoming relationship.

'Why don't we shower and then go grab some dinner?'

Jack narrowed his gaze at her, looking for more signs of her real feelings. She'd been awfully friendly all day, too friendly given all the issues he'd just counted up that were hanging over their heads. Still, he wasn't going to complain. Maybe she'd realised it was all trivial compared to how they felt about each other.

No such luck.

That much was clear within minutes of them ripping into some steaming hot naan bread in the town's Indian restaurant. All it had taken was for him to try and explain the phone call but he was pretty sure he'd done a rotten job of it. Judging by her reaction, he'd only explained the bad news, not the good.

'What do you mean, you can't tell management to give me the go-ahead?'

So he'd been right. She had intended to wow him today, back him into a corner so he'd *have* to approach management for her. He leant back in his chair, seeing how the fire in her eyes flashed as she talked. Boy, oh, boy, she was attractive when she was angry.

'What would have happened to Katie if I hadn't been there today?' She didn't wait for his answer. 'She'd be sleeping in the street or drift off to the city and fall into goodness only knows what sort of trouble.'

'What did—?'

Lauren steamrollered over the top of his question. Maybe he'd find out later what had happened to Katie. Or maybe not.

'You're going to *be* management shortly so why can't you fix it now?'

'It doesn't work that way, Lauren, and you know it.' He pushed his fingers through his hair. He felt a thousand years old right now. 'One of these days you're going to have to learn to work with the system. You can't just bulldoze your way through life.' He drummed his fingers on the tabletop. Why had things become so complicated between them? It had all seemed so straightforward when he'd decided to win her back. But he hadn't counted on life getting in the way. 'We've gone over all this. Can we stop and work through it like adults?'

'What do you propose?'

'I *have* talked to management and they've given you permission to keep doing one group a fortnight, for no more than an hour and a half, until a formal decision is made. I'll talk to the staff affected. You're all to submit overtime claims for that extra time.'

'I guess that's better than nothing.'

'And I think I can tell you that on first reading they were impressed with your submission. But that doesn't mean it'll be successful.'

She sniffed. 'You haven't explained about your job.'

Round two! 'I wanted to know exactly where I was with it first. But with your dad's accident and your submission, there hasn't been time.'

She started to talk but he held his hand up. He loved it that she was fiery and passionate, but this was one time she'd have to hear him out. Although for the life of him, he couldn't think of worse circumstances to tell her what he had in mind. Could the timing be any worse? It was almost guaranteed she'd throw it back in his face.

He took a chance. He reached across the table, pushing the basket of bread aside, and took her hand in his. There was reluctance written all over her face but at least she didn't pull away.

'This isn't exactly how I imagined talking to you about this, but I wasn't planning on disappearing on you. I want you to come with me.'

'To Adelaide?'

'Yes.'

'Leave my work, my home, my family? Just like that?'

'No, not "just like that". I was hoping it would be more like "It's what I've been wanting, too". You can't tell me our time together in Adelaide hasn't been on your mind ever since we left.'

'It was incredible but it wasn't real life. We didn't have to deal with any normal issues. It was a fantasy time. *This*—' she waved a hand around the room '—is real life.'

'What are you saying?'

'I'm not leaving.'

'I'm not asking you to give me an answer right now. But can't you promise to think about it?'

He could almost see the thoughts ticking over in her busy brain, but for the life of him he couldn't decipher them.

'I'll make a deal with you. Spend the day with me tomorrow and I promise to think about your offer.'

She sounded genuine so he dismissed the few nagging doubts niggling away. 'That sounds like a win-win situation for me. You're on. What are we going to do?'

'We're going to play tourists for the day. There's a lot more to this place than you've seen. We'll take your car.' She grinned at him and his trousers suddenly felt a tad tight in the groin. 'It's about time it got off the bitumen.'

CHAPTER EIGHT

As Lauren reached into the shower and turned on the taps, the thoughts that had been repeating themselves in her head since dinner last night spun around for the millionth time. What sort of a fool did Jack take her for? He'd waltzed into town, turned her life upside down and then calmly proposed that she hop up behind him on his horse and ride out of here into the sunset.

If she went to the city, she'd never have the freedom and level of autonomy she had out here, in her work or in her personal life. She'd miss the space, figuratively and literally.

Where else could she deal with the same range and scale of medical situations? It would be almost impossible to list all the scenarios she'd dealt with since joining the AAS. Not just emergencies—even the routine presentations had an element of the unknown due to the geographical distances involved. For someone who craved challenge, who liked to be kept on her toes, how on earth could any city posting compare? And what if there wasn't a vacancy with the AAS in Adelaide? Her next best option would be working as a midwife at one of the big public hospitals. Either way, she'd lose the variety that she so loved about her work now.

She threw her pyjamas into the corner and checked the water. Ouch. She turned up the cold water. The mild stinging sensation from the hot water faded but it'd take longer for the pain of a broken heart to disappear. And she'd never give up her dreams for love. It wasn't an option. Her words echoed around in her head.

Give up her dreams for love. Did she love him? She couldn't, she needed a country man. This was attraction, an affair, and she wasn't leaving for an affair. But she wasn't ready to let him go yet either.

That left her with one other option. The same one that had hit her between the eyes last night over dinner. Even after a night of mulling it over, it was still the only one. She had to make him stay.

Finally standing under the steaming jets of water, she made a mental diary for the day. The first day of her new operation, Operation Make Jack Stay.

She was still planning when she greeted Jack at the door. He was casually dressed in jeans and a white T-shirt and a smile broke over his face when he saw her. She couldn't be sure it wasn't her outfit making him smile. They were both in jeans but her T-shirt was lime green with purple trim, she was wearing an orange cap and carrying a bright red backpack. She shrugged. It hadn't put him off so far. And she wasn't about to start dressing for other people. Not at her age.

Lauren handed Jack her rucksack and followed him out to the car.

'Are we really going into the outback?'

'Don't look so nervous. We're going to the Flinders Ranges, which is technically the start of the outback. It's quite civilised and only a short drive.'

Jack laughed. 'I'm starting to realise that country and city folk have different definitions of short drives. What's this one?'

Lauren smiled, 'Two hours or thereabouts. But I will stop for morning tea on the way.'

* * *

Morning tea had been bought, consumed and almost forgotten by the time Lauren turned off the main highway onto a dirt road which ended at a camp site. Out of the car, she headed off along a dusty track, laughing when she looked over her shoulder to see Jack about to make himself comfortable at a picnic table. 'Come on, city boy, just a bit further.'

They walked without chatting. She loved this, walking with only the sounds of their footsteps snapping twigs and crushing dry grasses to break the silence of the bush around them. Stopping at a group of boulders, she chose a large flat one as a seat and tried not to wriggle closer as Jack sat next to her, their bodies touching, just.

She concentrated on pulling a Thermos from her backpack and pouring coffee, but she kept one eye and ear on Jack, watching for his reaction to this gorgeous place.

She heard him breathe in deeply and knew he must be smelling the eucalyptus in the air. Saw him look above them and knew he was following the flashes of pink and white as flocks of galahs took to the sky.

She nudged him as she noticed, above them on another rocky outcrop, two small animals, camouflaged by shadows.

As he turned his head to look, she said in a low voice, 'Yellow-footed rock wallabies. They're beautiful, aren't they?'

Jack nodded.

They sat side by side and simply watched the beautiful animals with large, soft brown eyes and an inquisitive air. Their distinctive striped tails and their coats were multicoloured, ranging from black to grey, white and orange. She could feel from his stillness that he was as fascinated as she with the sight of the wallabies hopping around the rocks, pausing to wash their faces and sample the native grasses. When they disappeared, the dappled light disguising their departure, it seemed as if the rocks had swallowed them.

'That was amazing, thank you.' Jack leant over and kissed her, and the wallabies were forgotten as he teased her mouth with a kiss that left her breathless.

He cupped her face with one hand and touched the tip of his nose against hers. It was an intimate, caring gesture and it left her with her heart turning slow somersaults.

'Where to next?'

'Wilpena Pound.' She coaxed her mind back to the campaign. 'We've flown over it on clinic runs, but to get perspective you need to see it from the ground.'

'"Wilpena" is aboriginal for "bent fingers"—is that right?'

Lauren raised an eyebrow in surprise.

'I'm not a completely ignorant city boy.'

'What else do you know?'

'The Pound is a natural basin, covering eighty square kilometres and ringed by steep cliffs. It's shaped like a cupped hand and that's where its name came from.'

She nodded. He'd done his homework. 'It's an important site for the Aboriginal people. There are some well-preserved artworks, mainly of the animals the locals ate, I thought we might have a look at.'

'Artwork that's been there for thousands of years.'

'Hundreds of thousands.'

He slipped his hand around the back of her head and rested it there, moving his fingertips gently through the softness of her hair. 'Then it can wait a few more minutes for us.'

She opened her lips slightly, the moment frozen in time. They hadn't come close to the level of intimacy they'd shared the night baby Cooper had been born. Would they now?

He dipped his head until their mouths were almost touching, and she lost herself in his nearness, her focus blurring as she looked into his eyes, until finally she felt her eyelids flutter closed as their lips touched. His kiss was slow, mingling with the heat of the sun, but she was sure of the source of the warmth enveloping her. She only ever felt like this with Jack, in his arms, with his mouth on hers.

But she couldn't succumb now. It wasn't the right time in her plan. Operation Make Jack Stay had barely got off the ground. Reluctantly she pulled away, ignoring his puzzled expression, and started to gather the remains of their refreshments.

They worked their way around the rocks, only letting go of the other's hand when the path became too narrow to walk side by side, trying their best to decipher the drawings. On the far side of the boulders was a narrow path leading further into the bush.

Jack stopped, pointing to the path. 'Where does this go?'

'Down to a very pretty waterhole. Are you up for a swim?'

'Is it OK for swimming?'

'If there's enough water, it's a lovely spot. Did you bring your swimming costume?'

'No.' He paused. 'Just my birthday suit. But that's nothing you haven't already seen.'

She laughed as he aimed a wink and a grin full of cheek her way.

'Don't flatter yourself. It's not me I'm worried about. What about all the poor unsuspecting tourists?'

Jack held up three fingers, mimicking a Scout salute. 'I solemnly swear to only swim in the buff if we're alone…'

He paused again and Lauren smiled, waiting for the condition she knew was about to be delivered.

'But only if you swim with me.'

He feigned a duck and weave as Lauren pretended to take a swipe at him before dodging past him down the path, calling over her shoulder, 'Last one in has to buy dinner.'

Jack caught up quickly and took her hand in his, slowing her down to a walk. As they approached the water-hole, Lauren heard other low voices, male voices, coming from the creek.

It looked like they wouldn't get their swim after all.

The voices were coming closer and Lauren saw three teenage boys, young men really, heading up the path towards them.

The boys raised their hands in greeting and started to move off the narrow path, making room for Lauren and Jack. As the boys stepped over sticks and small shrubs, Lauren saw movement out of the corner of her eye. 'Watch out!'

Her warning came a fraction too late.

One of the boys had stepped on a sun-baking snake, startling it into attacking. It happened so fast she could only watch as the snake sank its fangs into bare skin just above the boy's sneakers before he managed to shake it off.

'Kill it.'

'No!' Lauren's response was automatic and stopped the other boys in their tracks as they reached to grab nearby sticks. The snake disappeared into the long grass. 'Snakes are protected, you're not allowed to kill them.'

She didn't care that they all stared at her, no doubt thinking she was stark raving mad. She took charge. 'Sit down, keep as still as you can.'

'We need to know what type of snake it was,' Jack said.

'A Western Brown.' She turned to him. 'Can you run to the car and dig out as many long elastic bandages as you can find? You—' she indicated one of the victim's mates '—go with him to bring back the bandages.' She walked over to the victim while she spoke. 'Jack, radio the AAS and get them to patch you through to Wilpena Pound Resort. Get them to send someone to the car park with anti-venene.'

'That it?'

'Yes.'

As Jack and one of the young men left, she turned her attention to the others. 'I need you to find me a couple of strong branches, two to three feet long, an inch in diameter. We need them for splinting.' To the victim she said, 'What's your name?'

His friend answered. 'His name's Robbo. I'm Mark and Ewan's gone to the car.'

'OK, Robbo, you'll be just fine. The snake didn't have hold of you for long so chances are it didn't have time to inject much venom. The most important thing now is to keep still to slow down the spread. Are you having any trouble breathing?'

'No.'

That was a relief. He was looking OK at this stage, too, but the sooner Jack returned the better.

Mark came back with several long sticks, closely followed by Ewan with the bandages. Lauren took the gear from them and concentrated on bandaging Robbo's leg with tight wraps, working from the puncture marks down to the toes, then all the way up the leg to the groin. She was selecting two sturdy sticks from among the pile gathered when Jack returned.

'The anti-venene is on its way. What do you want me to do?'

'Lift Robbo's leg.'

Jack bent to do that and she gestured to Mark and Ewan. 'Can you two hold these sticks in place while I bandage them on to make a splint?'

Lauren worked at a steady pace while she monitored Robbo's breathing, and Jack lowered the leg once she'd finished.

'I asked for a stretcher and an oxygen unit. Was there anything else?'

She shook her head.

'Would you like me to wait back at the car park?'

What she wanted was for him to stay right there by her side, but it made sense for him to wait to direct the first-aid officer, so she simply nodded.

'I've already flattened the seats out in the four-wheel-drive to make room for the stretcher. I'll see you in a bit.'

He was right. It wasn't long before the first-aid officer arrived, and within ten minutes Robbo had been stretchered to the car, the oxygen mask over his nose and mouth, and the group was heading in convoy towards Hawker's hospital.

'We never did get that swim,' Lauren said as they left Hawker and headed south towards Port Cadney. She felt hot and grimy. No doubt she looked worse. She rubbed a hand across her face and could feel the dust caked into the dried perspiration on her skin. A swim would be bliss right now but it wasn't on the agenda.

'I don't mind taking a rain-check,' Jack replied. 'Unless, of course, you'd like to go back there now?'

'I think it might keep for another day. I have something else in mind.'

She shifted her gaze from the road to his face for a second and laughed when she saw the way his eyes had lit up at her comment. He was like a child on Christmas morning, full of anticipation.

'I don't think we have the same plans. Mine were along the lines of sipping a long, cool drink and meeting some locals. Or would you rather call it a day?'

'I'm not ready for the day to end just yet unless we're going home to bed.'

'My parents' station is on the way home. I thought we could call in there. My sister Steffi is there at the moment, too, with my niece Jess.' She held her breath, waiting for his reply. It wasn't a matter of being too soon—he was the one who'd asked her to move with him—but it was still a new stage in their relationship. Meeting the parents.

'You're willing to introduce me to your parents?'

'I'm game if you are.'

'Let's go, then.'

Jack nursed his beer as he sat with Frank Harrison on the back porch, watching the sunset, enjoying the quietness. Lauren's dad had suggested heading out for some air but Jack suspected he'd wanted to get him out of earshot of the three women inside. Four, if he counted young Jess.

'Can I ask you a professional question, Jack?'

'Shoot.'

'What can I expect to be able to do once my recovery is complete?'

So that was it. He felt the tension ease from his shoulders. He'd wondered whether Lauren had let them know about his proposal and he was in for a grilling. 'General daily activities should be no problem. Driving, some light farm work, golf, fishing, that sort of thing. But you should avoid heavy manual work, like fixing windmills and drenching sheep.'

'So there'll be a fair bit I won't be able to do, then.'

The note of resignation in the older man's voice was obvious. 'A lot of it you'll be able to do but you probably shouldn't do it.' Jack chose his words with care, not wanting to overplay Frank's loss. 'I'd guess that, on a property this size, a lot of jobs would take you the whole day. That requires stamina, and in my opinion it would be asking too much.'

Frank grunted. 'I thought you might say that. What about a hobby farm? I've been thinking it could be time to retire but I can't imagine doing nothing at all.'

'Depending how you set it up, that might be the perfect solution.'

'Margaret certainly thinks it is. I promised her years ago we'd move closer to the city one day. Maybe now's the right time.' He waved a roughened hand in the direction of his land around them. 'I probably could keep running the farm, with the station hands to do the heavy labour, but at some point we'll need to pack it in.'

'What will you do with the property?'

'Put it on the market. The girls aren't interested in running it full time and that's what it requires. Lauren won't be happy when she finds out. She's much more attached to this place than Steffi.'

'Lauren wouldn't want to take over?'

'She couldn't run the station and continue nursing. Even with her energy, it's too much. Margaret and I don't think she'd ever leave nursing altogether—she loves that just as much as the land, and she needs the interaction with other people. She's not one for lots of solitude.'

Jack hoped he was right. If Lauren wanted the land, if she had her heart set on keeping her parents' station in the family, there was nothing he could offer her to compete with that.

They took deep swigs from their bottles of beer, looking out over the paddocks, turning a burnt orange in the sunset.

Jack broke the silence. 'How will she take the news of the sale?'

'She'll come round. It'll be hardest on her and me, but we'll both get there in the end. Her mum and I might just need to lie low for a bit while she comes to terms with it.'

Jack laughed. 'You take that tack with her too, then.'

'It got us through her teenage years and I've come to the conclusion it's the only way. Let her go and she'll come round by herself in the end. Push too hard and she'll have her heels dug in so hard you'll never shift her.'

'Sounds familiar.'

'I'd appreciate if you don't mention this to her yet. We've still got a lot of thinking to do and it'd be better not to say anything until we've sorted out the logistics.'

'No problem.' Jack was quiet as he thought over Frank's words.

In the background he could hear the sounds of women's voices coming from inside the house. He hoped that if they were talking about him, Lauren had something nice to say.

'He seems lovely, dear. Is it serious between you two?'

'Mum! We hardly know each other.' Lauren grabbed

handfuls of cutlery from the kitchen drawer and started to set the table. She was starting to question the wisdom of coming here tonight—the questions had started flying the moment the men had left the room. And, at least while they were preparing dinner, she was a captive audience.

'From the way he looks at you, I think he's serious.'

She shrugged. 'He's asked me to move to Adelaide with him.'

Her mother paused in mid-rotation of the lettuce-spinner. 'And you said?'

'That I'd think about it. But I don't want to leave here.'

'Why not?' Steffi asked.

'I'm not going to pack up my life and move when all he's offering is a romance.'

'Would he stay here?'

Lauren shook her head as she slid the last few forks into place. 'He's more or less been offered a big promotion in the city. I couldn't ask him to turn it down on my account.'

'One of you…' Her mother paused while she gave the lettuce spinner an extra-vigorous turn. 'Might have to be prepared to compromise.'

'Uproot my life when he hasn't made any promises about a future together?' Mentally, she admonished herself. She wasn't about to sell out on her dreams, even if Jack made a thousand promises about the future.

'Love is about compromise.'

'Love?' Lauren said. 'No one's said anything about love.'

Her mother smiled. 'Have it your way, but we can still talk about compromise. Take your father and me, for example.'

'That's exactly my point. You compromised for Dad

and ended up in the country for ever when you were a city girl, born and bred.'

'I've been happy here, even though I'm still a city girl in my heart. But I love your father and he couldn't leave the station, it's all he knew. So if we were going to be together, I had to be the one to compromise.'

'You mean, give up all your plans.'

Her mother shook her head. 'Once your father retires, we'll travel and spend more time in town. That's always been our plan. I've just had to be patient.'

'Then look at Steffi.' Lauren pushed her hair out of her face with her forearm, her hands covered in juice from the tomatoes she was slicing, and waved the knife in her sister's direction. 'You moved to the city to keep your family together and look what happened.'

'I wouldn't blame that on our move. Rick and I wouldn't have lasted no matter where we lived, but I still don't regret the experience. Without Rick I wouldn't have Jess. And, speaking of Jess, I'd better go check what she's doing.'

As Steffi left, Margaret pushed the drained potatoes over to Lauren and remained standing by her side, her arm resting around her waist. 'Compromise has never been your strong point, darling. You get that from your father.'

Her mum gave her waist a squeeze to soften her words and Lauren leant her head against her mum's. 'But there comes a time when it's your only option. Of course, only you can say when that point is reached.'

'But I don't want to move. I'm happy here.'

'But will you be as happy here once Jack's gone?'

Lauren concentrated on mashing the potatoes. She was afraid she knew the answer to that question all too well.

CHAPTER NINE

'You've been awfully quiet since we left the farm,' Lauren said to Jack.

'Too full of your mother's cooking.' He took a hand off the steering-wheel to pat his stomach. 'I wouldn't want to get used to it or I'd soon not fit into my clothes.'

They drove in silence for a while before Lauren asked, 'What did you think?'

'About your parents?'

She nodded. 'And the station and my sister. You haven't said much.'

'I'm still digesting it all.' He glanced at her and laughed. 'No, I'm not just talking about that fantastic meal. It's a whole different way of life out here. I know I've been to stations before for work, but I got a different perspective today. Especially talking to your dad. He loves the land, doesn't he?'

'Now you know why Mum had to move out here. He'd never have left it.'

'Never?'

'No. Mum's told me they'll move to the city one day when he retires, but quite frankly I can't see it happening.'

'Why?'

'I know you've only just met him, but can you honestly see Dad pottering about in the city?'

'There are happy mediums, surely.'

Her quick glance and narrowed gaze told him he'd

almost said too much. He had to tread carefully here, not give her parents' plans away.

'What do you mean?'

He shrugged. Perhaps it was better to feign ignorance at this point. 'There must be ways for them both to be happy.'

'Such as?'

'I don't know. I've only just met them.'

'Whereas I've known them for ever, and I can't see it happening.'

It was on the tip of his tongue to ask her whether she couldn't see it happening or whether she simply *chose* not to see it. But today had been a good day, no, a great one, and he wasn't about to blow it by getting into a discussion that pushed her buttons. He changed the subject instead.

'Your niece seems a lot like you.'

'In what way?'

'She had me tumbling on the lawn with a ball and the dog within five minutes of meeting me.'

'You're right. I was just like her at that age. Energy to spare. All the Harrison females are like that.'

He moved his hand from the steering-wheel to rest it on her knee, and it was all he could do not to stop the car and take her in his arms. He put his hand back on the wheel and his mind back on the conversation. 'Where's Jess's dad?'

'He drifts in and out of their lives but he's never been a constant presence. I think he had good intentions, but having a baby straight out of high school was too much for him.'

'Is Steffi the reason you became so involved with teenage mums?'

'A big part of it. I saw how hard it was with family

support. Imagine what it would be like without it. That's why I can't give up those clinics.'

Jack turned into Lauren's driveway just as she finished talking.

'I can see how important a support network is.' But he wasn't about to agree that she was the only one who could provide it. He cut the engine and undid his seat belt, getting out of the car to open Lauren's door. 'I've got an early start tomorrow.' He gathered her in close and dropped a feather-light kiss on her forehead. 'And some sleep wouldn't hurt. But—' he dropped another kiss on one eyelid '—I'll sleep better—' he moved his lips to her other lid '—if you promise me you're still considering my proposal.'

She nodded, turning her face up to his, and he dropped a fourth kiss on her lips, barely brushing his lips across hers. The lightest touch could set him on fire. Even thinking about touching her could drive him to distraction. So he had to leave now, before he couldn't make himself go. The last thing he wanted was to make her feel pressured. But the first thing he wanted was to pull her into his arms and hold her close.

Instead, he saw her to the door, although it was some moments after she'd closed it before he could force himself to leave and go to his car. What he really wanted was to follow her inside and hold her close, and to hell with everything else. But Lauren was unpredictable. Plus, there were her father's words of wisdom to bear in mind, too. If he pressured her, it'd probably backfire and where would that leave them?

Lauren closed the front door and leant her back against it, her head spinning with thoughts of Jack. Wasn't she spontaneous? She always had been, until now. People certainly told her she was, so why was she hesitating? She would normally be the first to tell others to follow their hearts, but that would mean giving up her dreams. Jack had to stay.

No matter which way round Lauren looked at the problem over the next few days, she could still see only one solution, except in the wee small hours when she lay alone in bed and could almost feel Jack's touch on her body. Then she knew she wanted to be with him wherever he was, at whatever cost, but in the sanity of daylight she knew she'd be stark raving mad to throw her career, life and home down the proverbial toilet on a whim. Because he'd be giving up precisely what in return? Nothing.

Three, four, five days passed with neither of them mentioning the issue. She knew why she was keeping quiet—she couldn't pressure him to change his mind. She was hoping he'd come around by himself, with her gentle nudging. Was he doing the same thing with her?

As they walked to the plane together after finishing a remote clinic, Lauren realised the same words were playing almost continuously in her mind, like a mantra. He had to stay. Jack had to stay. There was simply no other option because she wasn't leaving.

They reached the plane and Jack put his hand out, touching the small of her back, motioning for her to board ahead of him. She was conscious of his eyes on her as he walked a couple of steps behind. She bent slightly to enter the plane and slid into a seat halfway along the tiny aisle.

He settled himself opposite her and met her eyes, a hint of a smile turning his mouth up in the way she loved. All day, she'd been conscious of where he was in re-

lation to her, knew immediately when his eyes had been
on her. It was a feeling she liked very, very much. She
missed it on the days they weren't rostered on together.
As it was, today she'd revelled in having him nearby.
She rubbed her bare arms where goose-bumps of expectation had suddenly appeared.

It was almost impossible to imagine that in a few short
weeks, days like today would no longer exist. He'd be
gone, unless she was successful in her campaign to keep
him here.

As they buckled their seat belts, they turned to look at
each other, and the smile that had been threatening to
appear spread across his face. She felt the warmth right
into the pit of her stomach.

He'd only got more gorgeous during his time here, if
that was actually possible. She kept facing him as he
turned to look out of the window. Another good sign, she
hoped. She often caught him taking in the view of the
changeable landscape below when they were flying. She
took in the whole sight of him, his face now in profile,
imprinting an impression of him on her mind.

His skin had darkened with the sun so that now he had
a healthy glow. His hair was longer and starting to curl
slightly. If he'd been in the city, he would definitely have
had a haircut by now but the extra length suited him. It
was another clue that he was more at ease, that the country suited him. She resolutely squashed an intruding
thought that what was true now wouldn't necessarily be
true for ever. She had to admit that moving out here was
a big leap and not many people made the leap for good.
But *some* people managed it. Why shouldn't he be one
of them? She turned away, leant her forehead on the
small oval window and squeezed her eyes tightly closed,
trying to shut out the thought that, in the here and now,

Jack staying would also mean giving up his career plans. She was pinning her hopes on being more important to him than his next career move, but could she really expect him to turn down a job he really wanted? She knew he'd been offered the position but he hadn't accepted it yet.

She wasn't about to give up her dreams so she just had to hope he didn't have quite such a tight grip on his own.

Lauren whipped around from the window as she heard Jack calling her. She was surprised to see him in the cockpit now. She hadn't noticed him leaving his seat. She undid her seat belt and went up front.

'What's up?'

'We're being diverted to Kingoonya to see a six-month-old infant with severe diarrhoea and fever.'

'And dehydration?'

'Probably. I know it's something you don't need me for but—'

'We've got you captive so you'll just have to delay that beer,' she finished off for him. 'What's the mum's name?'

'Jodi Matthews. She seemed relieved that it would be you coming.'

'You know Jodi. She was one of the mums in my group at Pimba.' She peered over Jack's shoulder at the map he was reading. It only took her a second to locate Kingoonya, one hundred and fifty kilometres from Pimba and three hundred and fifty from Port Cadney. Somehow it seemed to reinforce the need for her groups, seemed to prove that if Jodi couldn't get herself to urgent medical help when she needed it, she certainly couldn't ever get the other kinds of support she, Lauren, was looking to provide.

'How about you check baby Luke and I'll take care of Jodi? I imagine she'll be upset. Since we're both on board, we may as well both be useful.'

'Sure.'

It was only a simple thing, only a straightforward example of the fact they were able to work smoothly together, but she couldn't help but think it counted for something, showed how well he'd fitted in to the less hierarchical world of outback medicine.

It took another half-hour before they had landed and were off the plane. They'd asked the AAS base to track down a resident at Kingoonya to pick them up from the airstrip and now they were being driven to Jodi's.

Jodi opened the door and Lauren guessed she was struggling to put on a brave face. But her bravery dissolved the moment Lauren slipped an arm around her shoulders and told her they'd take care of her little boy.

'He's had a temperature and a runny tummy for a couple of days. Mum's away and I didn't want to bother anyone. But then I thought something was really not right, he's so…'

Lauren could see her trying to find the right word. 'Flat?'

Jodi nodded and Lauren squeezed her arm. 'Never feel it's too trivial to call us. Anyway, we're here now so let's let Dr Montgomery see little Luke.'

Jodi led the way across the room and stood next to her son's crib where Luke was lying, very still and very quiet.

Jack bent over him and peeled back the light wraps that covered him. 'OK, little man, what've we got here?' His voice was almost a croon and, despite her concern for the baby and his mum, Lauren couldn't help think about how appealing the sight of Jack leaning over *their* son's crib would be. Get a grip! she admonished herself as she switched the lever in her head back to work mode.

'What's he been having to drink, Jodi?'

'I breast-feed him, and I've been trying to give him water, but he hasn't wanted anything much at all since yesterday. He's not at all interested in food either.'

Lauren kept Jodi talking, getting the history they needed as Jack picked the little boy up and laid him on the change-table on a soft towel. He positioned a digital thermometer in Luke's ear.

'Nearly forty.'

Lauren wasn't surprised to hear the reading was almost forty degrees Centigrade. Even though the reading had only taken a second, it had been a tell-tale sign when Luke hadn't protested at all.

She watched and listened as Jack removed Luke's clothes with gentleness, telling Jodi what he was doing and then asking, 'Lauren, can you get some cool water and paracetamol?'

'Is he too hot?' Jodi was almost wringing her hands in front of her. 'I could've given him a bath before but I thought I'd make him too cold.'

'It's OK, Jodi, you did the right thing calling us and if we didn't know a few more tricks than you then we'd not be very good at our jobs. Can you help me by getting a bowl of lukewarm water, not cold, and a cloth or sponge?'

Jodi nodded and Lauren went on, 'Do you know how much Luke weighs, so I can measure out the paracetamol?'

'Six and a half kilos. I'll be right back.'

As Jodi left the room, Jack straightened up from the change-table and said, 'Textbook gastroenteritis. Fever, diarrhoea, loss of appetite. But…' He motioned to Lauren for her to complete the picture.

'It's not the gastroenteritis that presents the major risk to an infant but the resulting dehydration.'

'And again we've got a textbook case.'

Lauren had also seen that Luke's eyes appeared sunken and his extreme listlessness was also obvious. Now she watched as Jack pinched the skin on the back of Luke's hand and it failed to spring back into place. He moved his hands over the baby's head and skull.

The little rush of air Jack expelled told her what he'd found even before he said it. 'Sunken fontanelle.' He lifted Luke up and turned him over, gently turning his limbs, checking his armpits and groin with extra care. 'But at least his skin's clear of a rash.'

As Jack finished his examination, Lauren measured the correct dose of paracetamol, then held the little boy's face in one hand and slipped the syringe into his unprotesting mouth, pointing the tip into the cheek and pressing the plunger slowly to expel the liquid.

She continued to hold Luke's little face until he'd swallowed the dose.

Jodi came back into the room carrying a bowl of water and a cloth and in tears again. 'I couldn't find a clean cloth.'

'It's OK, Jodi.' Lauren took the bowl and cloth from her and started to bathe Luke with the tepid water while Jack took over with Jodi.

'You'll need to come back to town with us. Most likely, Luke's had a gastro infection, probably due to a virus. It's left him dangerously dehydrated.'

'But he's only been off drinking for less than a day!'

'It happens really quickly with babies, especially in

this heat. You did the right thing to call us and now the next step is to admit him to hospital.'

'Hospital?'

'He needs a special solution to rehydrate him and I want to run some blood tests to confirm exactly what we're dealing with.'

Lauren saw Jodi's look of horror but stood back to let Jack handle her. She didn't want to see it in quite this way, but she knew she was testing him whenever they worked together to see how he'd do as a country doctor. And so far she had no reservations.

'It's not so bad. The drip line will hurt a bit as it goes in, but it'll pick his levels up much more quickly. I'll start the drip now.'

Lauren hoped he'd find a vein on his first attempt. Jodi was already pale enough and really didn't need to watch more than one attempt to get a Jelco into her son's hand. She was glad when the line went straight in. And that Jack was sensitive to Jodi's fears, taking the time to explain and comfort.

'What are you going to give him?'

'It's just water with a mix of glucose and salt to replace what he's lost. Little ones at this age can't afford to lose a lot of fluid and Luke's had a bit of a battering with a fever, the diarrhoea and the heat wave.'

Jodi bit her lip and nodded her assent. 'Should I pack some things?'

'Good idea. Do you want Lauren to help while I get the drip up?'

In less than twenty minutes Luke was settled in his mother's arms for the flight back to town. Lauren hooked the bag of fluid up high and sat across from Jodi to monitor the flow. Her thoughts turned again to her work and the uniqueness of what she did for a living. How could she leave it behind? It wasn't just that a move to the city would impact on the scope of her nursing, there also simply wouldn't be the same sense of community that she had here. How often had she been called out to help people she knew? There were lots of little things that made her job here special. Maybe a city job would offer new challenges, but right now she couldn't think of any that would make up for what she'd be losing.

The day Jack would leave drew closer and then was almost upon him. He had one more day left at work, and unfortunately he wasn't rostered to spend it with Lauren. But if he hurried, maybe he could catch her before she left on a call-out. He had an ace up his sleeve that, if luck was on his side, might be enough to convince Lauren the city was the place for her. They'd somehow avoided mentioning the fact he was about to leave. The talks he'd had with her father over the past few weeks when they'd visited the farm had all reaffirmed that leaving her to come to her own decision to move was the only path to take. Trying to convince her would only do the opposite. She was pretty much like him in that regard. Stubborn. He respected that. And it wasn't like they had to rush—she didn't need to leave the minute he did. She could come later. But he hadn't really counted on her not saying anything at all by the time his bags were packed.

Luck *was* on his side. She was still at the base, standing motionless with her back to him, teaspoon in one hand, sugar in the other. She looked…distracted? Hope soared.

'Lauren.'

She rubbed her eyes and cleared her throat and it was further affirmation that he had reason to hope.

'Morning,' she said. 'How does it feel, knowing this is your last day with us?'

'Last day in this role, not last day with the AAS.'

'Semantics.'

'At least I can go out with a bang.'

She raised both eyebrows in silent query.

'I've got some good news about your proposal.'

'The funding has come through, they've OK'd it?' It was clear from the light in her eyes how much this meant to her.

'And then some. You've also got yourself extra funding for a psychologist, doctor or whoever you need to attend your groups.'

Lauren covered the few metres between them as though she had wings on her feet, and threw her arms around him. 'Thank you, thank you, thank you.'

He wrapped his arms around her and hugged her tight. 'You're welcome, but there's nothing to thank me for. It was your proposal. Your baby.'

'All the same, thanks for your help. I can't wait to get this back up and running. I've got so many ideas.'

He lightened his grasp on her and stepped back. 'There's something else I want to talk to you about. I know it's not really the time, but—'

'Go on, I'm not leaving for the clinic run for a while yet. Matt's been called in to the hospital so we can't go until he's back.'

'I know these groups are close to your heart and I understand now why that is.' He was choosing his words carefully and knew he probably looked like he was about to ask something he knew he shouldn't. He pressed on. 'You know I'm leaving in a few days.'

It was a statement. Of course she knew. She nodded.

'And I meant it when I asked you to come with me. I don't want to be without you.'

'Then don't go.'

'Pardon?'

'Stay here, with me.'

'I can't stay, Lauren, you know that.'

'And *I* can't go.'

'That's what I was trying to say, and I know I'm not making the greatest sense, but you *can* go. You can do just as much good in the city as here. You've got your victory now for your groups, you can leave on a high and hand over to someone to continue what you've started. You wouldn't be letting them down. And moving doesn't mean giving up on your desire to right the wrongs of the world. There are just as many people in the city who need someone to fight on their behalf, to believe in them.'

He could almost see the whirlwind of thoughts rushing through her mind as she bit down on her lip, frowning. This wasn't how he'd imagined this conversation.

'I know no one is irreplaceable but here I'm about as close to it as I can get. Who else would do what I'm doing? It's almost impossible to get professionals out here, particularly ones who intend to stay and also give a damn about this place.' He saw from the frustration in her eyes that he was included in that statement. 'Whereas in the city there are plenty of people to stand up and fight.'

'Sorry to keep you waiting…' Matt stuck his head around the door.

Lauren almost pounced on him. 'I'll be right there.'

Matt couldn't make himself scarce quickly enough, but the comical sight of his eager departure didn't raise a smile from either of them.

Jack blew out a deep breath and closed his eyes for a second. They were both frustrated and, no doubt, she, too, felt like she was banging her head on a brick wall but surely she could *see* why he couldn't stay, whereas she could so easily leave?

'And one other thing,' she said, clearly taking her chance while he remained quiet. 'The work as a flight nurse based in the city is vastly different to the work I do here. In Adelaide, we're not the first point of contact. Most of the work involves retrievals and there are very few true emergencies. And we don't get the autonomy or responsibility like we have working from the country bases. I don't want to give that up, that's one reason why I'm still out here.'

He looked at her for a long moment before he spoke again. 'I shouldn't have raised this here.' He could see her point but didn't he count for anything? 'Can we take it up later?'

Lauren shook her head. 'What's the point? We're coming at it from completely different angles.'

'So let's talk again and see what we're missing.'

'Matt's waiting. I've got to go.'

There was a moment of hesitation and then he nodded, his sense of propriety about not keeping workmates waiting winning out over his desire to pull her to him and kiss her until she gave in and agreed the only solution was to go with him. But it seemed that was only the right solution for him. Not her. They were about as far apart as they could be, and it looked like he'd be leaving town without her.

Lauren ground her teeth in frustration as she hurried to the tarmac. For once she didn't feel like facing a problem head-on. So shoot me. The thought that a bit of gratuitous violence wouldn't go astray ran through her mind. A good hard kick or two or three aimed at the plane tyres was strangely appealing.

She boarded the plane and strapped on her seat belt, thankful that at least she was in the cabin alone. Steve and Matt were up front.

Why couldn't she get through to Jack what the country meant to her? Clearly her tactic over the last few weeks of showing him just what a great life they could have here hadn't worked. It obviously hadn't even *occurred* to him that there was another option—that he could stay.

An odd feeling swelled in her stomach. Hopelessness? If she could have waved a magic wand to make it work between them, she would have. But if he wasn't prepared to stay, what other option was there? Long distance would never work if one of them didn't eventually intend to move. She'd give *anything* to make it work. Anything, that was, except give up her dreams. Surely that couldn't have been what her mother had meant when she'd said all relationships needed constant compromise and fair negotiation?

Within ten minutes of Lauren leaving for the clinic run, an emergency call came through to the base. They were minus one flight nurse today, struck down by a nasty virus, and Chloe was caught up with a difficult radio call, but Jack insisted he would manage solo just as the flight nurses usually did.

They arrived after a half-hour flight. Bill, a young English school-leaver on a working holiday, was suffering a moderately severe asthma attack. The station manager had no knowledge of Bill's condition so Jack had to get the information from the distraught patient.

'Do you have a history of asthma? Just nod or shake

your head,' Jack said as Bill opened his mouth to try and speak. Jack raised Bill's shirt and moved his stethoscope over a chest tight with wheezes. At least it wasn't silent, which would have meant the chest was so tight air could not even be expelled. Despite public perception of a life-threatening asthma attack being signalled by extreme wheezing, it was actually when it moved into the silent stage that a real emergency was occurring. Asthma at its worst was silent but deadly.

Bill nodded.

'Severe?' Jack started to get the medications ready.

Bill rocked his hand in the air, an action Jack took to mean he had problems only sometimes.

'Do you use Ventolin?'

Again, he nodded.

'Ever had hydrocortisone?'

He shook his head and Jack explained he'd be giving him some now to dilate his airways. He had no trouble obtaining intravenous access in the back of the patient's hand and quickly injected a high dose of hydrocortisone. He slipped the mask attached to the nebuliser over Bill's face and gave him Ventolin and oxygen for ten minutes. Checking Bill's chest, he decided another ten minutes was needed on the nebuliser, after which he found Bill had responded well.

'We don't know what triggered the attack so you'll need to come back with us so we can monitor you, at least overnight.'

Jack got no protest from Bill and figured he'd probably had enough of a fright to make him glad of the reassurance.

As they headed for the plane Bill explained, between mild wheezes, that he was asthmatic but it had seemed OK with his medication. He hadn't had such a bad attack for some years, although he used his Ventolin almost daily.

'I think we might have a better suggestion for managing your asthma. We'll probably put you on a preventative puffer, like Seretide. You shouldn't need to be using your Ventolin so much, and I think we'll find you don't once you're on preventative medication,' Jack said as he settled Bill in and then got himself ready for take-off.

He stayed monitoring Bill, only moving up front when Ryan buzzed him on the intercom to say he'd taken a call from Sheila.

'Is Bill stable enough for us to divert to a station about ten minutes from here?'

Jack got on the radio to Sheila. 'What are we looking at there?'

'Adult male with a deep wound in a calf muscle. It's bleeding heavily.'

'That'll be OK,' he said, when he realised the diversion wouldn't delay Bill's arrival at hospital for too long.

As Ryan flew over the airstrip Jack saw a flock of sheep in the scrub to one side. He pointed them out and Ryan did a second pass to scare the sheep further away from the strip.

How things change, Jack thought. Six weeks ago he wouldn't have given the sheep a moment's consideration. Ryan banked and approached for his landing. As the wheels touched down Jack saw a sheep happily tearing at some grass right in the centre of the strip. The plane veered wildly as Ryan tried to avoid it and that was the last thing Jack remembered…

CHAPTER TEN

LAUREN couldn't get off the plane fast enough. She'd been sitting up front in the cockpit when the call had come through that Ryan's and Jack's plane had crashed. They all knew take-offs and landings were more dangerous than any time during actual flights but somehow the risks had never seemed real. Until now.

'Steady on, Lauren. You have to wait until Steve has the steps in place or you'll be the next casualty,' Matt said. 'You let me run this, OK? Don't go getting hysterical on me.'

She made a sound of disgust but knew she'd already been less than professional since the news had come through, snapping at Steve to hurry up and get them there, hurry up and get the steps down. It wasn't what anyone needed right now, least of all the occupants of the crashed plane. What would they find?

She followed Matt out of the plane, her heart pounding furiously, adrenalin and fear running through her veins. What if—? But she couldn't think about that. Of course he'd be fine. She hadn't made the greatest mistake of her life, turning him down. There would still be time, she'd get another chance.

She saw Ryan, apparently unscathed, the moment she stepped out onto the plane steps, but from the way he was waving at them something was wrong. One look at the other plane confirmed her fears—the structural damage was considerable. And if she'd been in denial until now, she could deny it no longer. She loved Jack. If he was OK—dear God, please, let him be OK—then all that mattered was being with him. She started to run.

The sound of baaing seemed to be fading. It was an odd dream but even odder was the almighty pain in his neck. He must have slept on it wrong. He put a hand up to his head to massage the kink out, his eyes still closed.

And then realised he was sitting up. And wearing a seat belt.

What the—?

Jack opened his eyes and then it all came back to him, Ryan turning too sharply and flipping the plane while attempting to avoid a sheep. Lauren had been right on that count. Sheep *were* stupid, stupid creatures.

He quelled his immediate impulse to get out of his seat. He couldn't be sure he didn't have a major injury. A quick flick of his eyes to his left told him Ryan was no longer in the plane. Silence from behind suggested that their patient was either unconscious, had left the plane or was sitting, enjoying the view. Somehow he didn't think it was the last possibility.

'Mate! Don't scare the living daylights out of me.' Ryan reappeared in the doorway to the cockpit. 'You OK, then?'

'Don't move me. I'm not sure yet. But I think so. And as for not scaring people, perhaps you could keep the plane in a straight line next time. That might have had something to do with it.' He grimaced and rubbed at a sizeable lump on his temple.

'Cheeky bugger. Nothing wrong with your tongue, anyway. Steve and Lauren have just landed, detoured from the clinic run. Lucky they weren't far from here when I put the call through. And before you ask, young Bill is fine. Happily sucking on his puffer—' Ryan re-

ferred to Bill's Ventolin inhaler '—like there's no tomorrow.'

'Go and stop him before he passes out.' He closed his
eyes as a wave of dizziness swept over him. 'Or maybe
it's going to be me.' And then the world went fuzzy
again.

Ryan went to meet Lauren and Matt. 'The lad Bill's
OK—we were bringing him in for an asthma attack—and
I thought Jack was all right but I think he just passed out
again.'

Matt climbed the steps two at a time but turned to stop
Lauren and ask Ryan, 'What about the patient on this
station?'

'He's got a nasty gash to his calf but he's applying
compression and the bleeding has stopped. It'll need
stitching when you're through here.'

Matt touched Lauren on the arm. 'Check on Bill. If
he's OK, come straight up and we'll see to the stitching
last.'

Lauren opened her mouth to protest but Matt was right.
The potential for Jack to be more critical was clear, and
in that case he was Matt's patient. Her personal turmoil
didn't matter right now.

She checked Bill as quickly as she could, whipping
out her stethoscope to check his lungs and getting him
to blow into a peak-flow monitor to measure the air being
expelled on a number of strong breaths. It all looked re-
markably good in someone who had had a bad attack not
long before. Nothing else was required other than rest
and warmth, not a problem given the outside temperature.
'Wait here until we tell you otherwise. If you feel yourself getting worse again, call Ryan and he'll fetch me.'
She scarcely waited for Bill's nod before she took off for
the plane.

She came up behind Matt who was blocking the doorway to the cockpit with his bulk so she couldn't see Jack. 'How is he?'

Matt straightened up and turned to face her but made a noncommittal sound and Lauren's heart sank. He reached out and stopped her as she tried to push past him. 'Go easy, he's had a nasty crack to the head. I've fitted a neck collar as a precaution but I don't expect we'll find anything to worry about there. It's all come up fine so far. But like I said, he's taken a fair wallop to his head and had at least a brief loss of consciousness. He's still a little out of it.'

'Is that a medical term?' Jack's somewhat raspy voice sounded, the hint of laughter suggesting he would, as Matt thought, be fine.

'Don't you doubt it. I'll leave you with Lauren. I need to check the station hand.'

Lauren stepped forward into the small space just vacated by Matt and knelt down beside Jack, resting her hand on his. 'How are you really?' What she wanted to do was fling her arms around his neck and have him hold her close, reassure her he was really OK, but the neck collar was a reminder to be careful with him. Not to mention the less than friendly terms they'd parted on this morning. He might not want her anywhere near him.

'Put it this way, I don't feel any more beaten up than I did after our "talk" this morning.'

'Would you be serious?'

He laughed. 'I *am* being serious. I'm still a little fuzzy around the edges and I won't be asking you to dance in the next few hours, but, other than that, I think I'm OK. At least, once I've got rid of this damn collar.' He fiddled with his neck brace.

'Leave it on until we get you back to the hospital and let them be the judge of whether you're OK.'

He took it off anyway, dropping it to the floor. 'I don't need it. I had a brief LOC but my spinal column is intact.' He winked at her and her knees turned to jelly. 'Trust me, I'm a doctor.'

'That's exactly what I'm worried about.' She stood up, ready to help him to his feet, but was back by his side, hanging over him, the second he moaned.

'What is it?'

He'd closed his eyes and she felt the rising panic as he became very still.

'A kiss.'

'What?'

He opened one eye just a smidgen and she could see the mischief lurking there.

'I think I need a kiss.' A lopsided smile spread over his face. 'From you.' He took hold of her hand. 'Call it medicinal.'

'You're a scoundrel.' But she was laughing. He'd promised to get her back one day for her teasing. He'd certainly chosen his time well. 'And we have things to talk about.'

'I agree.' He took hold of her hand. 'Like how I'm about to kiss you.'

In an instant all her reservations crashed. She knew they had things to discuss but how could she even think about that right now? Her body was still running wild with adrenalin from thinking she'd lost him—and then realising she hadn't.

With a gentle touch he pulled her towards him and she couldn't resist. Who cared if there were still matters to discuss? Every fibre in her being was responding to his call and she followed it, lowering her mouth to his until their lips met and the sparks danced behind the lids of her closed eyes. All the pent-up anxiety she'd suffered since hearing of the accident crashed through the barriers between them and threatened to overwhelm them both. Fear, passion and relief flooded through her. At first only their lips were touching but when Jack slipped his hand around the back of her neck and eased her down to him, Lauren almost fell, so quickly did her body respond to him. Her knees were suddenly unable to support her and she sank onto his lap, wrapping her arms about him and meeting the increased urgency of his kisses with an honesty she found almost frightening, so little control did she seem to have over her feelings for him.

A knock on the fuselage stopped them short.

Matt was back. And he was grinning like a Cheshire cat. 'Feeling better, then, Jack?'

'I'll do, mate.' He paused as Lauren clambered off his lap. 'And you'll keep.'

'How's the station hand?'

'Nice change of subject, Lauren.' Matt laughed. 'He's fine. A bit of Betadine, some fancy needlework and a tetanus shot. He'll go in to the clinic at William Creek next week so we're right to go. How are you going, Jack? Think you'll be OK to walk yourself to the other plane?'

They were the last three onto the plane and it was a full flight by the time they had two pilots, two patients, Matt and herself on board. Just another in the list of factors conspiring to make sure this wasn't the time or place to tell Jack how she felt. She'd positioned herself in the seat behind his deliberately so she could see him but he couldn't turn to see her, couldn't watch her as her mind went crazy. A sensible move, because all she wanted was to be by his side but her mind stopped working when she did that. And she needed to make sense of what had happened today.

She looked out of the window but for once was hardly aware of the stunning view of flat lands rising in the distance to peaks of gold and green. She had some things to reconsider. She couldn't deny that when she'd heard the news of the crash she'd been filled with terror. The knowledge that, if the fates were kind and Jack was OK, she wouldn't just be able to let him walk away had hit her squarely between the eyes for the first time. But that didn't mean she'd just give in. She wasn't so daft that she'd let *him* know that they had to be together, no matter what. Not yet.

Her feelings for him were so much deeper than she'd been prepared to acknowledge before. Had she been scared of what it might mean?

She closed her eyes tight. They needed to talk but she had to make sure that she wasn't about to follow her heart and make the biggest mistake of her life. She wasn't at all sure if she could trust her head not to be hoodwinked by her emotions. Because she still didn't know if he felt the same way. If he did, wouldn't he have told her? She needed another adviser. Her mum? Chloe? No, they were all too busy with their own lives right now. She needed Steffi. Steffi especially could be trusted not to let her heart run away with her head.

She ran through her plan. Jack would be taken to hospital and Matt had already made it clear he'd be admitted overnight, despite Jack's complaints. Whereas she still had a day's work to finish before she could talk to Steffi. Five o'clock wouldn't come soon enough.

Steffi was already inside, opening Lauren's front door for her before she could get her key out. She stepped aside and let Lauren enter, kissing her on the cheek.

'Hi, there, sis. I gathered you need a talk so I have everything we need, ready to go. Including peace and quiet. Jess is with Mum and Dad.'

Lauren tossed her bag on top of a pile of objects on the table in the tiny entrance hall and led the way into the kitchen.

'It's pretty messy, Lori,' said Steffi, wrinkling her nose and looking around. 'We should have a tidy-up day while I'm here.'

'We're about to have a tidy-up day for my life as a whole, that's what I needed you here for.'

Her sister pretended to roll up her sleeves. 'That's what I'm best at. That and making snacks.' She indicated a platter of fairy cakes and biscuits on the kitchen bench.

'Cooking with my gorgeous niece again?'

Steffi nodded. 'What do we need to tidy up first? You? Jack? Your relationship? Both?'

Lauren shook her head. 'No, *all*.'

'Hmm.'

'What?'

Steffi pulled out a stool and sat down and Lauren followed suit.

'That was reflective listening, to show you I'm hearing what you say. And *you're* meant to feel encouraged to spill the beans. Come on, you're the one who's done the extra counselling training, you know how it works.'

Lauren shook her head. 'Just stick to the usual sister routine, OK?'

'Sure. What's up?'

Lauren laughed. 'Now, that approach I can cope with. Jack was in an accident today.' She hurried on when concern flashed across Steffi's face. 'He's OK. I've just been by the hospital on my way here and he was asleep. He's staying in overnight, but he'll be fine.'

'But when you heard about the accident, you thought he wasn't.'

'Yes.'

'And how did that make you feel?'

Lauren growled at her sister. 'You're doing the counselling thing again.'

Steffi leant back against the bench and nodded slowly. 'And you feel angry when I do that?'

Lauren grabbed a gingerbread man from the tray and tossed it at her sister. '*Stop* it.'

Steffi was almost sliding off the stool with laughter. 'Sorry, but it can't be as bad as you're making out. You look so mournful! How difficult can it be? You're both crazy about each other, he's a great guy, so get on with it!'

Despite herself, Lauren was smiling. It wasn't her style to be melodramatic, to wallow in her problems. 'OK, point taken. But I wish it was as simple as you make it sound.'

'Why isn't it?'

'It was only supposed to be a brief affair. You know, when you meet someone and there's instant attraction and if you were in your normal environment you'd never do anything about it 'cos there are too many sensible reasons not to? But when you're away and you both know it can't last, then you decide to just take the opportunity.'

'What do you mean by brief affair? When did all this start?'

'Remember when I went down to Adelaide last year for that midwifery refresher course? Jack gave one of the lectures on neonatal resuscitation. That's how we met.'

She paused, waiting for Steffi to admonish her for not telling her this before, but Steffi appeared dumbstruck by the revelations.

'He was gorgeous, so…male. He looked strong and capable but he was so serious. Then he laughed at some silly comment and his whole face lit up. He's got that dimple on his right cheek and he has this wicked gleam in his eye when he's amused. It floored me.'

'What happened?' Steffi appeared to have recovered her power of speech.

'I thought up a tricky question, one I knew the answer to but would take some time to explain. Then I suggested that he come to the pub for a drink with us all and explain it there.'

'And?'

'And we just clicked. We couldn't stay away from each other. We had a bit of a fling. No questions asked, no promises, no strings attached.'

'That was a bit impulsive, even for you.'

'I know. But Sarah and Sean had just got married, you were flat out with work and Jess, Margie from nursing had just had a baby. Everyone was settling down, whereas Ryan and I had broken up and I really didn't see us getting back together. I just wanted to feel young and carefree. And then Jack walked into the room and it suddenly seemed possible.' She paused for a moment, remembering again the first moment she'd seen Jack and her world had momentarily stopped. 'It was fantastic. *He* was fantastic. It was a brief affair and it just sort of happened. I never expected to see him again, certainly not here.'

'And now he is here. Why is there a problem?'

'I'm still attracted to him and I can't begin to describe how I felt when I heard about the plane crash. But I have to get over him. We're heading in different directions.'

'That's not true. You've got plenty in common—your

work and tennis, you light up in each other's presence, you laugh together.'

'But I want a country boy. I want to live here and he wants me to live in Adelaide. He won't consider staying here.'

'Which do you want more? Him or the country?'

'I want both!'

'Adelaide isn't far. Can't you work something out? Have a house up here for holidays?'

'Now, that is the very, very last thing I expected to hear from you, Steffi Harrison.'

'Why?'

'I thought you'd talk me out of it, tell me no man is a good risk.'

'Is that why you wanted me to come over, instead of someone you thought would say, "Go for it"? You *want* to be talked out of it?'

'Yes. No.' Lauren held the sides of her head and pretended to scream. 'I don't know. What do I do?'

She wriggled in her chair as her big sister fixed her with an unwavering look. 'What was your first thought when you heard about the crash?'

'That he was gone and I'd missed my chance to be with him. I felt as if I'd lost part of myself.'

Steffi stood up and took Lauren's hand. 'But he's not gone. Now all you have to do is ask yourself one question. "When I'm sixty, will I regret not taking a chance with Jack?"'

Lauren's response was automatic. 'Yes.'

From the look on Steffi's face, she'd startled both of them with her definite answer.

'There you go, then.'

'How can it be that simple?'

'If it's right, how can it not be?'

Lauren gaped at her sister. This wasn't what she'd expected. Except that now she'd said it out loud, it *did* seem that simple.

'Don't forget, the country will always be here for you. But if you turn him down, Jack won't.'

Steffi's words resonated through Lauren but she didn't have a chance to reply before her sister went on. 'And maybe it's all for the best, given that Mum and Dad are selling up.'

'What?'

'Oops. You still didn't know?'

'That they're selling? No, of course I didn't know. When? How? Who to?'

'No one yet, it's not been advertised. They would've told you before they did that.'

Lauren huffed.

'Really,' Steffi continued. 'Dad just couldn't face explaining it to you at the moment. He's got a lot on his mind and I think he was worried he wouldn't be able to go through with it if you got on his case.'

Lauren blinked away tears. She was surprised that she didn't feel anger. She felt...grief? She knew her parents were getting older and things would undoubtedly change, but she'd never thought that would mean selling the farm.

Steffi took her hand and squeezed it tight. 'It had to happen sometime. They're getting older; it's Mum's turn in the sun. You knew it had to come.'

Lauren drew her brows together and looked at the floor as if she'd find the key to her confusion on the ceramic tiles.

She'd always thought she'd be a country girl for ever, through and through. Now it seemed the fates were conspiring to make sure she never set foot in the country again.

But she couldn't deny that her conversation with Steffi had made one thing undeniably clear. Against all her instincts, the biggest risk for her was not that she'd lose the country—it was that she'd spend the rest of her days regretting that she'd lost Jack.

CHAPTER ELEVEN

JACK woke in the middle of the night disorientated and uncomfortable. He sat up in bed and waited for his eyes to focus. Gradually his vision cleared, although it was a little blurred around the edges. Rubbing his head, he looked around for some water. Seeing a jug next to his bed, he poured a glass and swallowed two painkillers that were waiting in a small paper cup beside the water jug.

He lay back on the pillows and waited to drift off to sleep but that proved difficult, his thoughts turning irresistibly to Lauren. In a roundabout way it was because of her that he was lying here. If he hadn't met her he would never have come to Port Cadney and he probably never would have considered branching out from emergency medicine into a career with the AAS. All in all, it was funny how much his life had changed since they'd met.

He'd always been focused on his career and he knew that, as a consequence, he'd lost touch with just about everything else. He hardly ever accepted social invitations, he was always too busy with work. Come to think of it, invitations were scarce now. His friends probably didn't even bother to include him any more, knowing they'd always be turned down. As for dating, he'd been even less enthusiastic. He simply hadn't wanted the distraction. But then Lauren had come into his life. Suddenly she'd been all he'd been able to think about.

They'd known when they'd met that their time together would be limited. They'd also known they'd snatch every

173

minute they could, so intense had been their mutual attraction. Lauren had only been in Adelaide for four weeks before returning to Port Cadney and he'd been leaving for a six-month study trip to Canada at the same time. The definite end to their time together had meant he'd been happy to enjoy their affair. She was like no other woman he'd ever met and, after all, one month couldn't be too distracting.

How wrong he'd been.

She'd made him laugh, made him enjoy life more than he had in a long time. Maybe ever. Her love of life was infectious and she was so stubborn. She wouldn't listen to his excuses about being busy and he found to his surprise that he didn't want to give her any. He *wanted* to spend time with her. She never seemed to need sleep and when he was with her neither did he. They existed on adrenalin.

She left Adelaide a few days before him. Time dragged. He couldn't wait to catch his flight out of Australia. Everywhere he looked he saw things that reminded him of her: a restaurant where they'd had dinner; the pub where they'd gone for a drink on that first night; a tall girl with dark hair walking down the street. He could clearly remember the disappointment he'd felt when she'd turned around and had been a stranger.

Arriving in Canada hadn't helped at all. He'd found he hadn't needed physical triggers to remind him of Lauren, he'd had the memories. That was when he'd realised he couldn't let her go, he had to see her again. So he had, for the second time, followed his heart to be with Lauren. And where had that got him? Here he was, recovering in hospital and still no word from Lauren about their future. Was there any? Her concern for him after the plane crash was promising. Maybe the accident would help to convince her of her feelings for him. He was almost sure now that she loved him, but even if he was right, was her love of the country stronger than her feelings for him?

If that was the case, what could he do? Jack's thoughts drifted, the painkillers were making him tired and vague now. But this was too important, he *had* to force himself to concentrate. He focused on the door, willing himself to stay awake as he mentally listed everything the city had to offer. Finally, just as the sky was starting to lighten with the approach of dawn he drifted off to sleep, having made some more promises. To himself and Lauren.

Jack's sleep had been brief, disturbed by ward rounds in the early hours of the day. And since he'd woken he'd been watching the minutes tick by until it had been a respectable enough hour to start making phone calls. He'd been flat out since then. He was a planner, Lauren had that right. And his plans always worked. He needed to get all the pieces into place but he was certain that Lauren would be his in the end. She had to be.

'That's excellent news. I look forward to seeing you.' Jack replaced the phone as Lauren came into the room.

If she'd overheard his conversation she didn't mention anything. She'd come to collect him. He was more than capable of getting himself back to the doctors' quarters but he hadn't been about to refuse her offer of help. They still had unfinished business.

They kept their conversation on safe topics as Lauren pushed his wheelchair around to the doctors' quarters. He'd tried to refuse the chair but had let Lauren have her way when she'd stated, quite firmly and with a big grin, that hospital policy said patients must be wheeled out on discharge.

And it was probably a wise policy, he had to admit, because by the time they were back at his flat he was feeling quite tired. Lauren took one look at him and made him lie down. He didn't argue and he enjoyed lying there, watching her fly around the tiny flat, opening curtains, making him comfortable. It wasn't a side to Lauren he'd seen before, although he suspected she was buying time as much as she was fussing over him. But once she'd made cups of tea and made him swallow his painkillers, there wasn't much more she could do. They had to talk.

He held out his hand. 'Come and sit down.'

She sat next to him, leaning against his shoulder. He kissed her hair. 'There are some things I need to say to you.' He pressed his fingers to her lips when she started to talk. 'Hear me out. You know I came to Port Cadney to find you. To find you when I realised I'd made a big mistake when we went our separate ways. If I hadn't been so lucky in that crash yesterday I might have lost you again for good. I don't want to risk it a third time.'

She nodded. 'I know. I've made a decision.' She moved away from him, raising her legs onto the couch and swivelling in her seat so they were facing each other, with nowhere to hide. 'I'm coming with you.'

'To Adelaide?'

'I'd sort of hoped for a more enthusiastic response.'

He could see her body language change. She was sitting taller now, holding her shoulders more stiffly. This wasn't going the way he'd been planning.

'You don't sound all that thrilled.'

'Of course I am. I just…I never thought you'd change your mind.'

'I have. Have *you* changed your mind?'

'About being together?'

'Yes.'

'No, I haven't.'

She visibly relaxed a little, some of the tension easing out of her body. 'What is it, then?'

'I've been watching you over the past few weeks and I've seen how much you love it here. You were right when you said that people here need your help.' Jack paused, running the back of his hand across his eyes. His head was throbbing but he had to try and sort this out. There'd been too much wasted time already. 'I thought your work might be more important to you than our relationship.' He needed to know how she really felt about him. She'd never told him in words.

'I thought it was, too, but there'll be other challenges waiting for me in the city. Yesterday made me see I have to take a chance. I couldn't believe I'd been about to let you walk out of my life. I don't want to spend the rest of my life wondering "what if?"'

Jack could feel fatigue coming over him as he fought to take in all Lauren was saying. 'You'll give up your clinics for me?'

'Someone else will take over now we've got funding. Besides, as you said, people in the city need help, too. I'll put in an application on Monday for a transfer to the Adelaide base. I'm sure it won't be too much of a problem.'

He felt his eyelids drooping as the painkillers took effect. There was still so much to say but he couldn't seem to form the words.

'I think our plans might have to wait. I'll get you a quilt, then I'll go and let you sleep.'

He felt her lay the quilt over him and brush her lips over his cheek and he fought the painkillers so he could tell her all he had to say, but he knew he was fighting a losing battle.

*   *   *

Lauren's phone rang early next morning.

'Lauren speaking.'

'Hi, sweetheart, it's Dad.'

She'd spoken to him and her mum last night on the phone and they'd made their peace about the decision to sell the farm. It still hurt but she'd accepted that they couldn't run it for ever and she herself couldn't do it alone.

'Morning, Dad. What's up?'

'We've had an offer on the farm. Your mother and I wondered if you wanted to take a look at it.'

Lauren was stunned. She hadn't expected things to happen so quickly.

'I'm not sure if I'm ready for this. I've only just found out about it!'

'It's a good offer, sweetheart. If we turn it down it might be a long time before we get another one. We haven't even had to advertise. Why don't you come out here and we'll talk about it?'

As she drove to the farm, Lauren fought with a tumult of emotions. It was one thing to decide to leave the country when she'd been able to envisage part of her life still here. And she'd made her decision and knew there was no going back. She had to be where Jack was. Couldn't imagine life without him. But it would take some time to get her head around not being able to come home any more. Not being able to sit on the porch with her mum and sister, drinking homemade lemonade. Not being able to ride out with her dad to check fences. Not any of it, not any more.

Her heart was in her mouth as she pulled up in front of the old house, like she was already starting to say her goodbyes. She'd just stepped onto the back porch when she heard another car coming up the drive. Turning, she watched as Jack's four-wheel-drive stopped next to her car, and she stepped back down from the porch as Jack opened his door.

'Should you be driving?'

He gave her a cheeky smile. 'I've never felt better—must be the good news you gave me yesterday.'

He kissed her and she kissed him back before remembering why she was there. Moving away, she said, 'It's not a good time right now. Mum and Dad have had an offer on the farm and I'm here to have a look at it.'

'I know.'

'What do you mean?'

'It's my offer.'

'Your offer?'

He nodded and her jaw dropped. 'You want to buy the farm? Why?'

'For you.'

'Me? What am I going to do with it? I'll be in Adelaide with you.' Lauren paused. She'd been right yesterday, he had changed his mind. 'You don't want me to come with you any more?'

Jack laughed and took her by the hand, stepping up with her onto the porch and pulling her down to sit by him on the wicker couch. 'Of course I do, but I don't believe you're ready to let go of the country completely. This way, you don't have to.'

'But I can't run a station from Adelaide. I couldn't even do it from here unless I gave up my nursing.'

'I realise that. I've spoken to Sean Fitzpatrick, he wants to buy the sheep and lease the land for pasture. It's a perfect solution. You get to keep the homestead and a parcel of about ten acres, plus the income from leasing the land. Sean's been looking for some agistment land as his property isn't big enough to make a good living in these dry conditions.'

This was happening too fast. 'But I won't need the homestead. We've talked about this. I'm applying for a transfer to Adelaide.'

'I know, and I appreciate it. But I think, if you're honest about it, you're not certain.'

Lauren recalled Steffi's idea of spending weekends in the country. Adelaide wasn't *that* far away after all, and Jack obviously thought it could work. But Jack was still talking.

'And I haven't been quite honest with you.' He shifted back on the seat and turned her shoulders so they were facing each other square on and could see each other's faces clearly. 'I want us to make our life here.'

For once she was speechless.

'Do you remember the day we met?' he asked.

She nodded.

'I can't remember a word of my lecture but I remember everything about you. You were wearing a bright pink T-shirt and your hair was down. Your arms were tanned and you glowed. You looked so healthy and full of life, I couldn't take my eyes off you. You've been consuming me ever since.'

His gaze roamed over her face, settling on her lips, and she felt as though he was kissing her without touching her, such was the expression on his face.

'I haven't been able to get you out of my head and that's an amazing thing for me. I've always been so focused but that focus has, without exception, been directed towards my career. The moment I met you, that all changed. My career started to take a back seat to you, but that was so strange to me I managed to deny it even to myself. Until the crash.'

Lauren opened her mouth to say something but he held a finger gently against her lips and continued, 'Let me say this. I came to Port Cadney to find you, and I promised myself that I wouldn't leave without you. For a while there it looked as though I'd lost you and it finally hit me last night. If you wouldn't leave, I'd have to stay.'

'But I've said I'll go with you. You don't need to do this.'

'I know, and that's what makes this so right. I don't *need* to, but there's nothing I *want* more. Come here.' He eased her head down onto his shoulder and started to run his fingers through her loose hair, each caress leaving her almost breathless with contentment.

'There's nothing waiting for me in the city other than work. I never had time for hobbies, I barely had time for an occasional social tennis game, I hardly ever went dancing and I saw my friends once in a blue moon because I was always too busy.'

To Lauren's ears he was describing a fairly miserable existence but she twisted her face up to watch him and he was smiling. She was stunned and wondered whether he was really saying what it sounded like. How could things have changed so quickly?

'You told me on my first day here that country life was special, if I would just let myself experience it. I didn't think it could be so different but I feel as if I've really been alive here, for the first time since you left Adelaide. There *is* more to life than just working. I know that now. And I know I can't ask you to give up your life here for a life in the city, a life that *I* don't even want anymore.'

'But what about your promotion?'

'I was going to turn it down.'

'You can't.' She'd intended to convince him to stay

here and it seemed she had. But surely he'd regret making this sacrifice? 'It's too important to you.'

'Not as important as you are. We wouldn't be *as* happy in the city. No job is worth more than you are to me.'

'I can't let you do that.' Lauren paused. Now that she had what she wanted, she was feeling scared. What if she'd really forced his hand and he just didn't know it? Would he come to regret his decision? 'Why don't we try living in Adelaide first? It might be fine.'

'I don't want fine, I want what we can have here.'

He put his arm about her and pulled her closer, but she pulled away slightly. She'd never be able to believe this wasn't a dream if she didn't watch his every expression as he talked to her. She needed to have a visual record. She made do with resting her palms on his chest instead, spreading her fingers out so she could feel as much of him as possible beneath her hands.

His gaze met hers and she melted all over again.

'As I said, I *was* going to give up the promotion but it turns out that's not necessary. I spoke to the CEO and he's agreed to a trial period of working from Port Cadney. There are enough return flights to Adelaide when I need to go to the city.'

'Are you sure you're OK?' Lauren looked bemused, reaching out to touch the bruise near Jack's temple. Another problem occurred to her. 'You might still be concussed.'

'I told you, never better. It's the country air.'

He *sounded* like he was OK. In fact, as he'd said, he'd never sounded better. Could she, then, dare to believe what he was saying?

'You're ready to be a country boy?'

He nodded. 'You were willing to be a city girl for me. It's better for you this way. The role of a flight nurse based in Adelaide is very different to your current job. And, as you told me, this is your town and you bring something to it that no one else could.' He teased her lips with a light kiss. 'The city won't miss either of us but Port Cadney would miss you. And you it. You'd have been giving up everything to move for me.'

'But now you're giving it all up for me.'

He laughed and held her closer, one arm still around her shoulders, his other hand cupping her face, stroking her cheek with his thumb in the way she loved. 'No. I'm gaining everything by moving to the country.' Jack turned Lauren's face towards his, kissing her. 'I'm getting you.' He kissed her again. 'Hearing yesterday that you were prepared to move for me made me sure you feel the same way. Then I knew this was the only thing to do, the right way for us to be together.'

His eyes were filled with an expression of such desire that Lauren caught her breath.

'I love you, Lauren.'

Those were the words she'd been waiting for, even without letting herself admit it. Those were the words, she'd known since yesterday, that would've had her packing her bags weeks ago to be with him. 'I didn't know!' She could hear the wonder that was flooding through her spill over into her voice. 'You never said before.'

'I didn't know there was a time limit.'

They smiled at each other and she saw the same happiness she felt written all over his face, his broad smile, the laughter in his eyes.

'I admit, I've been slow in realising what was staring me in the face. It didn't really hit me how I felt until you told me that you weren't coming with me. Told me so in no uncertain terms, as I recall.'

Lauren closed her eyes and squirmed. 'Sorry about that.'

'It was nothing I didn't do to you, too. I have a sneaking suspicion that we're both rather stubborn. And then, of course, there was the crash, and that could've ended very differently. Then there was no denying it. But I'll tell you again to make up for my delay. I love you, Lauren Harrison, and this farm is my present to you. My wedding present.' He got off the seat and knelt before her, still holding her hand in his as he asked, 'Will you marry me?'

The question she'd not dared to dream about hung in the air between them. Could this really be happening?

Lauren looked into his eyes and knew that, yes, it was definitely happening. She stood and put her other hand out to him, and he stood, too, catching her in his arms to enfold her in an embrace, caressing her mouth with a kiss that dispelled any lingering doubts about his love for her.

As he lifted his lips from hers, he said, 'This is one question I do want an answer to today. No more weeks and weeks of us dancing around each other, not talking about what really matters.' The twinkle in his eyes softened his ultimatum. 'So, is it yes or no?'

'It's yes. From the bottom of my heart. I love you.'

'I have to warn you, there'll be no changing your mind. Remember, I'm every bit as stubborn as you are.'

'Do you think that's a problem?' She could ask that now she knew it would never be anything but a source of passion and respect between them.

He entwined his fingers with hers. 'There'll never be a problem that will threaten my love for you, there'll never be a wind strong enough to shake what we've found.'

She laughed up at him, her love and her heart suddenly large enough to share with the whole world. How could she not have known until today that there was a happiness as pure and joyous as he'd given her?

'What are you thinking about, my sparkling, beautiful wife-to-be?'

'Whoever thought my country man would come striding into town disguised as a city boy?'

'Not you, I'd guess.'

She wrapped her arms about him so she could whisper, 'I always did like surprises.'

As he bent his head to hers, she closed her eyes and felt the whole world tilt and right itself as he found her mouth with his in a kiss to seal the gift of a lifetime. With love from him to her.

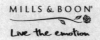

BETTY NEELS

DEBBIE MACOMBER

JESSICA STEELE

A classic
Christmas
collection...

Christmas to Remember

On sale 5th November 2004

*Available at most branches of WHSmith, Tesco, ASDA, Martins,
Borders, Eason, Sainsbury's and all good paperback bookshops.*

...Michelle Reid
.....Jane Porter
...Susan Stephens...

One
Christmas
Night

On sale 3rd December 2004

*Available at most branches of WHSmith, Tesco, ASDA, Martins,
Borders, Eason, Sainsbury's and all good paperback bookshops.*

MILLS & BOON®

Live the emotion

Tender
romance™

THE AUSTRALIAN TYCOON'S PROPOSAL
by Margaret Way *(The Australians)*

Bronte's had enough of rich, ruthless men – she's just escaped marrying one! So she's wary when tycoon Steven Randolph arrives on her doorstep with a business proposal, especially as she finds him impossible to resist. Only then she discovers that Steven is not all he seems…

CHRISTMAS EVE MARRIAGE by Jessica Hart

The only thing Thea was looking for on holiday was a little R & R – she didn't expect to find herself roped into being Rhys Kingsford's pretend fiancée! Being around Rhys was exciting, exhilarating…in fact he was everything Thea ever wanted. But back home reality sank in. Perhaps it was just a holiday fling…?

THE DATING RESOLUTION by Hannah Bernard

After a series of failed relationships, Hailey's made a resolution: no dating, no flirting, no men for an entire year! But what happens when you're six months in to your no dating year and you meet temptation himself? Jason Halifax is sinfully sexy and lives right next door. What's a girl to do?

THE GAME SHOW BRIDE by Jackie Braun *(9 to 5)*

Kelli Walters wants a better life – even if that means participating in a reality TV game show. She has to swap lives and jobs with vice president Sam Maxwell – telling people what to do while he has to scrape by as a single mum! But Sam soon ups the stakes with his heart-stopping smiles and smouldering glances!

On sale 5th November 2004

4 FREE

BOOKS AND A SURPRISE GIFT!

We would like to take this opportunity to thank you for reading this Mills & Boon® book by offering you the chance to take FOUR more specially selected titles from the Medical Romance™ series absolutely FREE! We're also making this offer to introduce you to the benefits of the Reader Service™—

- ★ FREE home delivery
- ★ FREE gifts and competitions
- ★ FREE monthly Newsletter
- ★ Exclusive Reader Service offers
- ★ Books available before they're in the shops

Accepting these FREE books and gift places you under no obligation to buy, you may cancel at any time, even after receiving your free shipment. Simply complete your details below and return the entire page to the address below. You don't even need a stamp!

YES! Please send me 4 free Medical Romance books and a surprise gift. I understand that unless you hear from me, I will receive 6 superb new titles every month for just £2.69 each, postage and packing free. I am under no obligation to purchase any books and may cancel my subscription at any time. The free books and gift will be mine to keep in any case.

M4ZED

Ms/Mrs/Miss/Mr ....Initials ....
BLOCK CAPITALS PLEASE

Surname ....

Address ....

....

....Postcode..................................

Send this whole page to:
UK: FREEPOST CN81, Croydon, CR9 3WZ